KISS OF DARKNESS

ALIEN VAMPIRE HUNTER

SHERI-LYNN MAREAN

Copyright © 2019 All rights reserved.

This book is for your enjoyment only. You may not sell, give away, copy, reproduce, distribute or transmit, in any form, (whole or part) by any means, electronic, digital, optical, mechanical, including photocopying, recording, printing, or any information storage and retrieval system, without prior written permission from the author. Any person who does any unauthorized act in relation to this publication may be liable to criminal prosecution and civil claims for damages.

OTHER BOOKS by SHERI-LYNN MAREAN

DRACONES: CURSED & HUNTED (52 Realms)

Primalthorn ~ Prequel Novella
Dragonsworn Guardian ~ Novella
Dracones Awakening
Dracones Revelation
Dracones Betrayed
Dracones Thaniel
Dracones Rogue
Dracones Guardian
Dance with Darkness
Defiant Wolf: Curse Breaker
Dragon Heart Awakened ~ Sanctuary Anthology
We All Gots Beasts ~ Return to Sanctuary Anthology
Beat of my Heart

DRAGON HUNTER BROTHERHOOD (52 Realms)

Saberthorn
Casstiel: Born of Lightning
Daggerthorn: A Christmas Gift Novella

LEAGUE OF SUPERNATURAL ASSASSINS (52 Realms)

The Dragon Assassin
League of Supernatural Assassins Shared World

ALIEN VAMPIRE HUNTER

Kiss of Darkness
Hunting Darkness

MATES OF CARMELOH

Fantasy Lovers

Never stop dreaming...

PRONUNCIATIONS

- Andrican: And rick ann/Vampire
- Antoli: An tole ee
- Alidonna: Ali donna
- Apolly: Ah polly
- Belsuma: Bel soom ah
- Beltin 1 Orian: Bel tin 1 or eye on
- Cain Orvey: Cain or vey
- Cherro: Chair oh
- Dadeus: Dade ee us
- Grem: Grem
- Harbinger: Har bin jer
- Indris Electa Kava: Indris electa kava
- Joem Artes Kava: Jo em art es kava
- Kade D Kava: Kade D kava
- Kellan: Kell an
- Kelseyann: Kelsey ann
- Mayara: May are ah
- Nico: Knee ko / novarian
- Novarian: Nov air ee ann

- Rafarious: Raf air ee us
- Rossa: Row sa / Andrican
- Sentinally: Sent in ally
- Viper: Vipe er
- Weren: Where en

1

Somewhere in Space

As Captain Kade D Kava made his way toward the flight deck, a communication flashed across the intergalactic comm unit strapped to his wrist. It stopped, then blinked again, letting him know it wasn't something he should ignore.

: Sentinally.

: The strange event called Halloween happens this day on planet Terra Nova.

: Weren ship en route to the human planet.

: Assistance required ... code urgent.

Of course it was, and why wouldn't it be? Just when he hoped for a minute's respite, something had to come up. As the message blinked repeatedly, Kade silently swore. Halloween? He vaguely remembered hearing something about the Earthlings' tradition of dressing up in odd costumes and knocking on strangers' homes at night. It had always seemed a rather silly, if not dangerous, act to him. Sure, it originally meant something else a very long time ago, but it no longer did for most Earthlings.

For a weren ship to be headed to the planet was sheer suicide, and as far as he knew, they weren't stupid. So then, what the bloody goalendamn was going on?

Kade tapped his wrist unit, and a holo-screen popped up with the face of a stunning redheaded female. "Lieutenant Kelseyann, you can't be serious."

"Kade D Kava. It's been too long." The lieutenant's smile dropped away. "I wish I weren't, but I really need your help."

"What happened to the *Dadeus*? They're supposed to be guarding the human planet."

"They went dark two months ago," she replied.

Kade raised an eyebrow. "Another ship's crew just gone?" The one guarding Earth before the *Dadeus* had also disappeared.

Kelseyann sighed. "This one lasted five years at least. Anyway, we've just been informed that a weren ship is en route to the planet now. They went to start a colony there."

"Why would they attempt that on Terra Nova?"

Kelseyann shrugged.

"They do have balls," he said. Weren, the wolflike shifters, topped the deadliest beings in all the galaxies. "Think it's the *Raken Claw*?"

"Honestly, I don't know," she answered.

"How sure are you of this intel?" Kade asked.

"It came from a trusted informant."

That wasn't what Kade wanted to hear. "And the emperor wants *us* to step in and what, eliminate the beasts and contain the fallout?"

Kelseyann hesitated. "Not exactly."

Kade sighed. "He has no idea you've asked me, does he?"

Kelseyann shook her head. "I can't reach him, and there's no one else even remotely close that I can call on. At least, none I trust to get this done properly."

On his way past the lounge, Kade glanced through the window to see a few of his crew hanging out and playing a tabletop war game. "You do realize I don't work for the emperor, right?"

"And you understand what'll happen if the weren attack isn't stopped, especially if this is the *Raken Claw*?" Kelseyann stared at him. "Or if news gets out?"

Kade knew all too well. Besides the fact that heads would literally roll within the emperor's army, others would see Terra Nova as fair game. Then war would break out. There would be many deaths, especially for the innocent beings on Earth. Even worse, if this was the *Raken Claw*—a notoriously known pack of rogue pirates—they'd been chasing, they had a lot to answer for. Like the death of one of Kade's hunters.

"Please, Kade. You know I wouldn't ask if the situation wasn't dire."

Kade stopped at the doors to the flight deck and waited for the retinal scanner to do its thing. "You want me to change course, knowing my men and I are all blood-drinking Andricans, and head to a planet of humans, who are completely ignorant of the multitude of alien beings in the universe?" Well, a couple were only half Andrican, but their other half—Regarian—were just as reliant on blood to survive.

Kelseyann cringed. "I'll make it up to you the next time I see you?"

"Damn right you will."

"Thanks, Kadey." Kelseyann blew him a kiss.

As the door slid open, Kade swiped his wrist unit and the screen with her image disappeared.

Double goalendamn. He didn't need this right now. He and his men had just come off a grueling, devastating stretch after tracking down and locating a vile bunch of grem. The oily-haired, greedy ratlike shifters were the scourge of the universe.

Kade wanted to give his warriors some badly needed time to rest. Refuel. Get their minds right after losing one of their own.

The death of a fellow hunter was always difficult. To lose a friend was even more challenging. And this warrior had been like a brother to all of them.

Kade entered the deck that was located at the front of the ship and gazed out the massive window at the stars. "Trace any weren ships en route to Terra Nova."

"Weren?" His number one pilot, an Andrican male with pale skin, a mess of long black hair, and dark-purple eyes, scowled up at Kade from his seat. "And Earth? Isn't that out of our way?"

Kade nodded. "It's the strange human custom called Halloween coming up, and apparently, a group of weren are about to enlighten the Earthlings to the existence of their deadly shape-shifting alien beings."

"Of course the wolfy astards are." Mayara snarled under his breath and pulled up the screen needed. "Halloween. Isn't that where the weak humans send their even weaker younglings out dressed as monsters to accost strangers at their homes and demand candy?"

"I believe you summed it up correctly."

"Stupid, or naive." Mayara's fingers danced over the keyboard in front of him. "I don't know why the emperor keeps the whole planet shrouded in ignorance. It's not like he fears the Earthlings."

No, that particular ruler didn't fear much. To him, Terra Nova was simply a slave stronghold of cattle made for his consumption. However, the emperor had been known to offer up a human as a bribe, often to curry favor with a high council adversary.

Kade had never agreed with how most of the powerhouses ran things, which was why he was a hunter and not in the emperor's employ.

"I've got one weren ship moving toward the West Coast of the United States. Los Angeles, California, to be exact." Mayara bared his fangs. "You think it's the one we've been chasing?"

Kade shrugged. "No idea. Probably not." It wouldn't be their luck. "Take us there."

"Oh joyous blood-spiked hairballs." Mayara set the coordinates for a new course, then leaned back and looked at Kade. "What happened to stopping for nothing until we reached Beltin 1 Orian? You know, to rest and feed?" Mayara raised an eyebrow.

Kade didn't like their change of plans, either, but the consequences would cost them all if the upcoming slaughter wasn't stopped. And maybe, just maybe, they'd catch a break and would learn the whereabouts of the weren pack they'd been seeking.

"Hey, Mayara, you ever taste an Earthling?" a male Novarian, one of four that made up the flight crew, asked with a gleam in his eyes.

Mayara narrowed his gaze on the male. "You know the law."

Three of the four were males, two of which were both mated to the same female, the crew's only female, in fact. Though they shared traits with humans, like body size and structure, that's where the similarities ended. A roving race, the Novarians had blue skin and were much more volatile and hardier. They tended to disregard laws, and those Kade had ever met lived to pillage, fight, and have sex. They took what they wanted in whatever way suited them best. Most were dangerous killers that even he would hesitate to cross.

How Mayara managed to rope them into joining the crew, Kade still didn't know, but he had to admit they were among the best pilots he'd ever come across. Still, he knew better than to ever completely trust them.

The threesome shared a smoldering glance. "Fun times ahead." The female grinned, then her tongue darted out to slide over her blue lips seductively. Only, it turned Kade off even more. He caught the eye of the fourth unmated male, the brother to the female, but with a wink, the guy went back to his screens.

As pilots, the Novarians would wait on board while he and his hunters took care of their weren problem, unless one was needed to pilot a craft. Otherwise, the three of them would spend their time in their quarters getting hot and sweaty. It was, after all, one of their favorite pastimes. What the fourth did, Kade didn't know, and didn't think he wanted to know.

As if he'd heard Kade's thoughts, the oldest mated Novarian male, this one with short white hair that stuck out at all angles, looked up at him. "Hot and sweaty lovemaking is a good way to lose yourself for a while. You should try it sometime."

Kade scowled. "I've had sex."

"You've done the act to release energy, but you've never had hot, sweaty, ball-clenching, toe-tingling sex." The male smirked before turning back to the panels in front of him.

He was right. As an Andrican, Kade could copulate to relieve stress, but that was all it was suitable for. As a male of his species, he could not feel more than a slight pressure when anyone touched him. He couldn't feel pleasure, pain, heat, or cold. The only way he could ever *lose* himself in the act was with a soul-bond mate. The rarest of matings. Something Kade didn't have and never would.

"You could join us sometime, Captain," the female with long blue hair offered with a sly smile. "We have gifts. We can make you lose yourself."

Mayara grinned.

"I appreciate the offer." Kade hid his shudder and took his seat.

Once the warp drive was engaged and they were on their way, Mayara focused on Kade again. "I know we all want to catch the *Raken Claw*, but the team needs to replenish their energy."

"We can feed on Earth when we're done," Kade said. "We'll just have to be quick and discreet about it." And hopefully not succumb to bloodlust.

"When we're done? Discreet? You're some kind of funny bunnycat today, Cap. You're killing me here." Mayara ran a tongue over one of his fangs. "Yup, we'll wait and feed on the most luscious nectar in all the galaxies *after* we chase the goalendamn weren furballs through a million human bonbons!"

Kade's gums ached, his own fangs throbbing at the thought. Human blood was said to be the sweetest anywhere. It was supposedly capable of setting even the strongest Andrican warrior on the edge of bloodlust. Which, besides the law, was one of the reasons he and his hunters stayed away from the human-bound planet.

No, his men wouldn't be thrilled with their next mission. It wouldn't be easy to be close to the hot-blooded, iron-rich meals and not slake their thirst. In fact, it would be pretty bleating hard.

But they were all well-trained warriors. Kade narrowed his gaze on Mayara. "They know their duty and what failure means. They can damn well control themselves and feed after they're done."

Mayara tilted his head. "What of the emperor? He won't be pleased to learn we've fed on his humans."

"Do I look like I care?"

Mayara smiled, and an evil glint flicked in his purple eyes. "Don't you?"

"This will be payment for helping save his pretty little planet," Kade snapped.

"And your sister?" Mayara asked.

Kade sighed. His sister was the reason they lost a hunter. "She can stay on the ship until we're done. I don't need her fucking anything else up."

"What don't you want me fucking up this time, big brother?"

Kade turned and scowled at the tall, lithe creature with long black-and-silver hair who'd just entered the flight deck. Adorned in a set of worn black leather pants and a skimpy halter top, she was a stunning female. Though the wild beast within her kept the males of most species from getting too close.

"Most" being the keyword.

Apparently, the grem weren't included in that category. Nor the weren.

The thought of how close the weaselly grem had come to delivering his sister to the weren set Kade's blood roaring. "I told you to stay in your quarters. Do I have to post a guard on you as well?"

"And I told you I had everything under control, but you don't listen. You just had to swoop in and *rescue* me," Indris hissed.

"That's because we've had this conversation before. You were in danger. I wasn't about to let you get hurt." His head began to pound.

Indris glared at him. "That's the thing, I wasn't in any *danger* and damn sure didn't need rescuing, and I refuse to be brought back home like some wayward child."

Kade ignored the last part. "The grem are cruel, greedy animals. Shifters of low intelligence, yet they had a plan to hand you off to the *Raken Claw*. What exactly do you think that pack of weren, who are more powerful beasts and of higher intelligence, would do with you?"

"They wouldn't have hurt me," she said.

"You don't know that. They're working with the grem, and are the reason I lost a hunter," he snapped.

"You don't know that the *Raken Claw* had anything to do with his death," she said.

"Again, they're working with the grem, need I say more? Besides, what does it matter, grem, weren, they're all without morals and can't ever be trusted."

Indris flicked her fingers at him. "You make them sound so horrible. They're not all like that, at least not the weren."

"They're even more dangerous than the grem. Those bloodthirsty savages wouldn't hesitate to hurt a female not of their pack." An exceedingly dominant race, what the weren would have done to her sent terror straight to Kade's heart. The grem would have used her, and hurt her. But he'd heard the weren liked to prolong torture until the person broke mind, body, and soul. "You're safe, so it doesn't matter now, does it? The wayward grem are on their way back to the Candor empire and their master, and after we make a stop, we'll head to Beltin 1 Orian so my hunters can feed. Then, I *will* be taking you home."

She paced around the flight deck for a moment. "Why can't you release me on Beltin 1?"

"This whole convo was old the first time we had it. I know you can't stand Father, but seriously, why don't you want to go home?" Kade asked. "He rarely ever comes by, and you know that Mom misses you."

"I miss her, too, but—" Indris glanced at the crew, who, she knew heard every word, kept their eyes on their consoles. She looked back at Kade. "I have something I need to do, and you set me back by *rescuing* me."

"You were held by beasts who don't care what happens to you." He was getting tired of repeating himself.

"I'm one of those beasts." As her eyes flashed silver, a faint ripple of white fur with black streaks ghosted across her pale ivory skin, revealing her mixed heritage. A betrayal of his father by their mother, and one that Indris loved to throw in Kade's sire's face. In the end, it landed her in the fucked-up dungshit they'd recently rescued her from, and cost them a good Andrican male.

"No, you are not. You're nothing like them and never have been." The suffering she'd endured during childhood for being different broke Kade's heart.

Though in defense, Indris had wrapped herself in a shield of anger, indifference, and defiance, and as she got older, she made their parents' lives a nightmare as often as possible.

Hands now tipped with claws, she slowly raked a strand of hair behind one ear as she gazed out the window. "We're in warp. Where are we going?"

"To take care of something."

Kiss of Darkness

"I thought we were on course for Beltin 1. What's going on?" At Kade's silence, Indris shook her head. "Another mission? Seriously?"

Kade wished, not for the first time, that his little sister would just do as she was told.

"Kade!"

"It's just a short one." He sighed. Why did dealing with her always have to be so difficult?

"A short one," she fumed. "Fine, I need to get off this tin box for a bit anyway." Her claws sprouted even farther. They were an extension of her that she used like weapons or when anxious.

Kade shook his head. "You're not coming. You aren't part of this crew, remember? I seem to recall you wanted nothing to do with us hunters."

"And because of my choice, you what? Plan to lock me up like the creatures in the hold?" Indris propped her hands on her hips. "For how long?"

Kade loved his sister, but there were times when she tried his patience. "You know I'd never put you in with them, but it would be better if you stayed in your quarters. Only for a short time. I promise, just until we're done."

"Done with what?" she asked again.

"We're chasing a weren ship," Mayara piped up.

Indris went still. "The *Raken Claw*?"

Kade sent Mayara a look before focusing on his sister. "We don't know, but you have nothing to worry about. You'll be safe up here."

"What if I want to help?" she asked.

"Not happening."

Silver eyes flamed with cold fire. "I'm not one of your precious hunters. You can't tell me what I can or can't do."

The pain in his head had turned into a full-fledged headache. He needed blood and an end to this conversation. "I'm the captain of this ship, and you're my guest. You will listen for once."

"Don't try to tame me, big brother. I'm not a lap cat."

"I know, Indi." Kade used her nickname. "I'm not trying to tame you or anything else. I just need you to stay here."

Indris started to say something, then stopped before she continued. "Where is it we're headed that you're so determined I not follow?"

They dropped out of warp, and a planet lush with brilliant blue water and vivid greenery appeared in front of them. Part of the world was shrouded in the darkness of night, though millions of little lights twinkled over the surface.

"Terra Nova?" Indris whispered. Her claws retracted.

"Yes. Now do you understand why I want you to stay here?" Kade asked.

Indris stared at the large forbidden globe known as Earth. A faint smile tugged at her lips. Then she turned and started for the flight deck door. "Sure, whatever you want, big brother."

Kade didn't trust the sudden mood change. "Indris?"

"This beast is getting out of your hair, just like you wanted." She waved her hand without looking back.

Kade scowled, aware she was deliberately pushing him. Yet it wasn't like her to give up when she wanted something.

"Sorry, I shouldn't have said who we were following," Mayara said quietly without meeting his gaze. "Thought maybe it would calm her, but that was just weird."

"It was." Kade stood.

Mayara looked up at him. "Want me to notify the team to meet in ops?"

"Yes, in twenty."

Kiss of Darkness

The weren would see Earth's strange custom as open season with no reason to use stealth or hide their true selves from the population. The silly humans would think they were in very well-made costumes, never knowing what hit them.

Still, the fact the weren wouldn't be hiding their werewolf forms would make Kade and his hunters' job of capturing the furballs easier.

Back in his quarters, Kade raked a hand through his short blond hair and met his blue-eyed gaze in the mirror. This task would test his hunters in ways they hadn't been in a very long time. Would his crew be able to hold firm against the lure of the humans? Would he? He was tired and hadn't fed in too long, and the last few times hadn't been satisfying. Was he close to going rogue?

Kade turned away and suited up, strapping on his weapons. He'd also been looking forward to some downtime, but now that would have to wait.

His comm unit buzzed.

"Cap, we've got escapees from holding block two on deck nine."

Kade swore. "How many and how'd they get loose?"

"All of them and no idea," the gruff voice on the other end answered.

More dungshit he didn't need. "Be right there."

Kade took the lift down to deck nine, where one of his men waited. A stocky, orange-haired, amber-eyed Andrican male named Rossa.

"We've managed to get most of the grem rats back inside their holding cell. Cherro and Antoli are sweeping blocks one and three, and Kellan is chasing down one slippery little bugger that disappeared into block four," Rossa informed him.

"And Viper?" Kade asked.

"He's—" Rossa didn't get to finish as a scream pierced their sensitive eardrums. Rosa snorted. "Looks like Viper got his prey."

The doors to block five slid open and a lean but muscular male emerged. With long black hair that was tied back and piercing blue eyes, Viper wasn't one to be messed with. As another piercing screech rent the air, he sent a fist into the face of his captive, knocking the grem unconscious. Then he proceeded to drag the rat along the floor behind him. When they chose to take on their two-legged form, the grem resembled humans, except they barely reached four and a half feet in height. However, they preferred their giant rat forms and rarely took on their human one.

A bloodthirsty race that tended to leave a trail of dead bodies in their wake, Kade had never dealt with the grem before. But their kidnapping of his sister and the subsequent death of his hunter changed all that.

"There's a pretty planet below us that looks nothing like Beltin 1 Orian," Viper stated, blue eyes ice-cold.

"There is," Kade replied, then jumped back as a panel in the wall beside him flew off and skidded across the floor. "What the helltar?"

A set of large feet appeared from the ventilation duct, then the rest of their fellow warrior.

Kellan, Viper's younger brother, only shorter and heavier, and without the hairy face, emerged.

"What are you all staring at? I got the little ankle biter, didn't I?" Kellan yanked a cussing, snarling grem in his two-legged form, out of the tube. As soon as the beast hit the floor, he shifted back into a rat, teeth snapping and claws swiping at Kellan. The hunter pulled his blaster and trained it between the wide-set beady red eyes. "Shall I shoot you now? I'm still pissed over your bunch killing one of my brothers, and I gotta tell you, I'd be more than happy to see your blue brain matter all over the floor, even if I have to clean it up myself."

The grem settled down immediately.

Rossa shook his head sadly. "Well, that's a shame. watching you scrub the floors would totally complete my day, Kell." He scanned his handprint, and the doors to holding area two whooshed open.

With his weapon trained on the grem, Kellan smirked. "Sorry to disappoint, Rossy." Then he directed his next question at Kade, though he kept his eyes on his captive as they entered the holding area. "Why exactly are we hovering in space above Terra Nova when we should be sipping some sexies on Beltin 1?"

"Halloween came up to bite us on the ass," Kade replied.

Kellan frowned. "Isn't that the stupid human—"

Kade nodded. "That's the one."

"And?" Viper asked.

"And, the weren decided the law regarding Earthlings no longer matters," Kade answered.

"They're on the way to Terra Nova?" Rossa asked.

"Likely there already," Kade responded as they neared the cell holding the recaptured grem.

Kellan growled. "Isn't this a problem for the *Dadeus*?"

"It would, if they were anywhere to be found." Kade scanned the grem inside, noting the beady eyes that stared back at him with hatred. He'd be glad when they dropped this lot back on Candor.

Rossa let out a low whistle. "Another crew's gone missing while guarding Terra Nova? That's not good."

It wasn't. Kade deactivated the cell lock.

Viper dragged his catch over to the cell. "This won't end

well." Then he tossed the mongrel in, leaving the door open for his brother.

Kellan waved his weapon. "Get your smelly furball ass in there with the others." As his captive slunk inside, Kellan holstered his weapon and looked at Kade. "You can't be serious. We're going to human-infested Earth?" He started to swing the cell door closed, then paused when Cherro and Antoli entered the hold.

Both of their escapees crept along the ground ahead of them, tails between their legs.

"What's this about humans and Earth?" Cherro asked, a light in his brown eyes.

"We'll discuss it in ops." Kade turned to leave, but hadn't taken more than one step when

one the grem Kellan had captured spun around and slammed into the door, knocking Kellan back. The grem grinned as Cherro and Antoli's pair rushed forward and launched themselves at Kellan, claws extended.

Viper shot one grem between the eyes, and Kade took the other out.

The two grem landed on the floor where they twitched for a moment, then fell still.

"Next?" Kade swept his gaze over the living rats, his eyes coming to rest on the one who'd charged the door. The male backed off and the rest of them remained still.

With a snarl, Kellan shoved the lifeless bodies of the ones who dared to attack him into the cage. "Just for that, the rest of you can spend your time in lockup with your dead buddies here. I'm sure they'll be nice and ripe by the time we reach your master." Kellan slammed the cell door shut, waiting as the lock engaged.

Kade holstered his weapon and surveyed his prisoners.

Kiss of Darkness

"There's no way off this ship for any of you until we get to Candor. Unless I decide to send your furry asses out an airlock. So, unless more of you want to die, I suggest you relax, hunker down, and tell each other fairy rat tales."

Most kept their eyes lowered, though the more daring grem glared at him, lips curling.

In the ops center, Kade updated his warriors of the pending weren attack on Earth they'd been tasked with stopping. "And before you ask, we don't know if this is the *Raken Claw* pack. Either way, it doesn't matter. The weren will be stalking humans, and we have to stop them."

A ripple of unease, followed by anticipation, had each hunter tensing. Eyes began to glow, and fangs dropped. The expectation of battle always set the blood pumping, but tonight's temptation was human blood. And the fear of bloodlust.

"None of us have fed in over two weeks." Kade met the gaze of each hunter. "Beltin 1 Orian was supposed to be our time to rest, relax, and refuel. But you all know that if the weren start killing Earthlings and reveal themselves to our existence, war will break out up here among the stars. Many of our friends will lose their lives. I know what I'm asking of you, so this mission is not mandatory. There can be no feeding until the weren have been captured or killed. If anyone decides to sit this one out, there will be no hard feelings."

All but Viper grumbled that they wouldn't miss this chance to take out the hated weren.

"Viper?" Kade asked his quiet friend.

"You think I'd stay behind?" Red lightning sparked in his blue eyes.

"Nope. Just wondering if you had anything to add," Kade said.

"I do." Viper swept all of them with a hard stare. "How'd the damn grem escape?"

"That's an excellent question." Kade was about to contact Mayara when his comm unit buzzed.

Everyone started to voice what they thought happened as he swiped his screen.

"Captain?" It was one of the male Novarians.

Kade held up a hand for quiet. "What is it?"

"Someone manually activated the override into the landing bay, then launched one of the single fighter ships out the hull doors."

With their enhanced hearing, his men followed the conversation.

Kade's stomach clenched. "Where's Indris?"

"She's not in her quarters; and, Cap, I don't have her location anywhere on the *Sentinally*," the Novarian said.

"Goalendamn!" Kade tapped his comm unit to end the convo.

"Indi jumped ship," Kellan stated. "You think she let the grem out as well?"

"That's a bloody good question." Kade had a sinking feeling she was the cause of the diversion, for it definitely was one.

"She wanted us occupied. Why?" Rossa asked.

"So she could go down to Earth." Kade snarled. "Damn female is going to get herself killed." If not by the bloody weren, then by him.

2

Earth Candy

ARMED WITH WEREN antivenom for the humans, and bristling with weapons, they boarded the shuttle.

From his seat at the helm, Mayara glanced back at Kade and the rest of them. "Ready?"

"As we'll ever be." Kellan grinned. "Let's go trick-or-treating on Earth."

Kade nodded as they all strapped in.

The hunters utilized their wrist units to learn more about Halloween, Earth, and its inhabitants.

"I told you all before." Kellan growled and rolled his eyes. "You should have listened to me and watched the *shows* I tried to get you to watch. They would teach you all you need to know about this world and its people."

Viper glared at him. "Enough about those silly shows you watch all the time."

"I want to see one," Rossa said.

"We don't have time for a full show, but here, check this out." Kellan sent a file to his fellow hunter's wrist unit.

"What is it?" Rossa asked.

"A movie trailer," Kellan said.

Rose watched it, then started to laugh. "I think I'm going to like these Earthlings."

"Told you," Kellan said smugly.

"Seriously?" Viper raised an eyebrow.

"You should try it. There's all kinds of stuff available, even —" Kellan pulled up another vid, and sounds of moaning could be heard. "Like this one, they aren't at all shy—"

Viper swiped his brother's wrist unit off.

Kellan glared at him. "Aw, what'd you do that for? I was having fun. You should try it sometime, loosen up, you know?"

"We're here, children." Mayara set their cloaked ship down in a valley between two hills.

"You found the weren vessel?" Kade asked.

"I did. In fact, it's right beside us, according to my scanner," Mayara replied.

Lights twinkled from homes a short distance away. "I'm picking up some small Earthbound critters, but no humans near us."

"Anyone on the ship?" Kade asked.

"I'm not detecting any life signs."

Kade drew his laser blaster anyway. "Better be prepared just in case."

His crew nodded and armed themselves.

The door to the shuttle slid open, and Kade and his crew set their feet on Earth for the first time.

"I don't think we're in Kansas anymore, Captain," Kellan

said with a smirk as they stealthily made their way over to the other ship.

No, they were not. The air was fresh and invigorating, unlike many other planets they'd visited.

Excitement shining in his eyes, Mayara used his unique, tech-based mental abilities and dropped the other ship's cloaking. "It's the *Raken Claw*." He practically purred at the sight of the high-caliber ship.

"Open her up and let's hope you're wrong about no one being inside, 'cause I'm in the mood for some weren." Viper growled.

Mayara concentrated, and the door in front of them slid open.

There was no one there.

After searching the ship, they all reconvened back outside.

"Nico, you ready to bring this baby back to the *Sentinally*?" Mayara asked the youngest Novarian on their crew.

"Absolutely." Nico grinned, just as much a tech nerd as Mayara.

As the others voiced their disgust over it being a weren vessel and possibly having weren disease, two of the furry creatures appeared on the trail not far away, noses to the ground.

They paused, lifted their heads, and at the sight of Kade and his crew, their eyes began to glow. They bared their teeth, saliva dripping from their mouths as they charged.

"This is what I needed! Bring it, bitches," Kellan yelled as he trained his blaster on the pair.

Viper took the lead beast down, and his brother got the second one, which elicited glares over the two stealing all the fun from everyone else.

As the beasts died, a swirling mix of colorful light rose from the bodies. Then they just dissolved.

"I see that you all got this under control," Mayara said as he returned to the weren ship.

"I'm going to scout around, see if I can find anything to shoot," Antoli informed Kade before misting away.

"Astard," Cherro said with envy over his fellow hunter's ability. "I'll track the weren from the ship, see if I can find out which way they went."

Kade nodded. He, Rossa, and Nico kept watch while the weren ship fired up with a barely audible hum.

Mayara emerged, eyes bright. "This baby is fine. I can't wait to go through her and learn what makes her tick." He nodded at Nico. "This sleek baby is ready to go."

"You got this?" Kade asked the male who was to pilot the weren vessel back up to the *Sentinally*.

Nico grinned. "Like a tasty piece of ass."

As the Novarian took off, Antoli reappeared. "The weren astards split up."

It was what they figured would happen.

"Keep in touch," Kade instructed his hunters.

Despite the daunting task ahead of them, there was a surge in adrenaline to be after their prey. Hunting other predators was what they did best, and it wasn't often they went after the formidable weren.

But then the wolflike shifters were smart and usually kept under any hunter's radar.

"Ready?" Mayara asked Kade after his hunters had melted into the shadows in search of their prey.

"Let's go." Kade got back in the shuttle.

Mayara delivered him to the ship that Indris had absconded with, then had hidden in a clearing surrounded by trees. "See you when the dungshit clears," Kade said as he once again set foot on Earth.

He caught Indi's scent and began to track it.

In minutes, he was in a subdivision where children, most accompanied by their parents, went from house to house, dressed in various outlandish garb.

Kade groaned. So many innocent beings were in the streets everywhere he looked. The scent of their sweet blood had his fangs throbbing with hunger.

Kade did his best to avoid getting close to the humans while keeping to his sister's trail.

Before long, he caught a whiff of weren and the aroma of blood. It wasn't the rich human blood, but rather weren and Andrican. More importantly, it was his sister's.

He snarled.

Well aware Indris was capable of taking care of herself, Kade still couldn't help the protective urge from rearing its head. She was his little sister, and if she'd been hurt, nothing would stop him from tearing the bastard responsible limb from limb.

He forced himself to calm down, then continued after the scent trail. It led between a couple of three-story buildings.

In silence, he crept into the alley, then halted.

The scent trail was suddenly gone. Not a drop left anywhere, not even the faintest tint of it.

But how could that be? She couldn't teleport.

He drew in a deep breath and held it, searching for his younger sibling.

Nothing.

Kade turned in a circle, eyes studying every nook and cranny. But it was as if she'd never been here.

Did his little sister have abilities she'd been hiding from him?

He went back out to the street and began to walk, but when

it didn't produce any results, he backtracked and went the other way.

He rounded a corner, and a group of six pretty human girls, around the age of fifteen or sixteen, approached along the sidewalk. Dressed up in costumes, they chatted and laughed, some digging into their bags of candy. A couple eyed Kade. The richness of their blood was enticing as it flowed hot in their veins.

After they passed by, Kade melted into the shadows. The brutal need for sustenance thundered through him. His fangs ached to sink into tender flesh. He waited until the hunger passed, and watched as four boys of about thirteen, who smelled like they hadn't bathed in a while, trailed after the girls. Though at an awkward age, Kade caught their desire to be noticed and realized that humans were easy to read mentally.

He was pondering that discovery when a gang of males, maybe eighteen or nineteen years old, neared. Unbidden, images of them stalking the girls filled his mind, taking away all thoughts of feeding.

Dark, disgusting scenes of what they wanted to do to the young females made him sick. They'd been stalking them for over an hour and now had a plan.

Kade emerged from the shadows with a growl. "You need to leave those girls alone."

The group of thugs turned to him.

"What the hell, dude? If you're going to jump out at people, you should at least be dressed up." Dressed all in black with a silver skull on his shirt, the speaker was of average height and medium build.

He considered himself the most intelligent in the group. Someone unafraid to tell it like it was, and he loved when the others laughed at his smart-ass comments, as they did now.

Another boy, this one wearing a white-and-black-striped

Kiss of Darkness

outfit, indicated Kade's weapons. "Maybe he thinks that's good enough for a costume." He met Kade's gaze. "What you supposed to be, some kind of space cop?"

"And who do you think you are telling us what we can or can't do?" the largest of the bunch in blue jeans and a black T-shirt asked, an angry sneer on his face. A deeper delve into his mind revealed his name to be Jory. And he was pissed at being interrupted in his chase of the girls. He also had the vilest intentions of the group.

Kade revealed the tips of his fangs. "You can call me your conscience or your worst nightmare. Your choice."

They snorted, and some laughed nervously, though a few inched back just a bit.

"Let's go," Jory said to his friends. "This asshole is a nutcase."

Kade blocked him.

Jory started to challenge him, but Kade held him immobile with his mind, then he swept his gaze over the rest of them. "Are you all as twisted as your buddy here?"

"What the fuck?" smart-ass skull boy asked, all humor gone.

"Don't worry. You don't have to answer. I can see it all. I just needed your minds open a bit more." Kade grinned as he utilized his Andrican ability. Then he pushed.

"What the hell, man!" Amid groans and cries, the group clutched their heads.

Kade walked away, satisfied. Anytime one of them even considered doing something horrible or perverted to someone else, they'd end up in excruciating pain.

He continued on and soon found himself on a busy street with restaurants, bars, and one particularly loud club. He shuddered at the noise.

Women and men passed him by, some alone, some in

groups. The next group to approach had a nurse, a witch, a playing card, and a male dressed as a bunny. The last costumed female looked as if she were trying to pretend to be dead. Or was it undead?

"Hurry up, Tally, you can call him back later," one woman said to another trailing after them. The one called Tally spoke into what Kade thought must be a human communication device. But it was her bright red high heels and slinky crimson dress that gave Kade pause and made his hunger surge once again.

The woman slid the device into her satchel, smiled at him, and then looked at her friends. "Go ahead. I'll catch up."

With knowing smirks, they continued into the place vibrating with music.

"You're not in costume," the woman named Tally said to Kade, her gaze traveling up and down his body. A glitter of appreciation in her eyes.

"You aren't either," he commented, homing in on the pulse of her neck.

She shrugged and laughed. "No, I suppose I'm not." Her hand landed on his arm. "Want to join us? My friends won't mind, and Halloween is the perfect excuse to party."

No, I want to take you to an alley and drink you. Kade moved away. "No, sorry, I'm looking for someone." He silently added that she'd have no idea what she'd be getting anyway.

The woman's lips formed a pout. "Oh pooh! Well, if you change your mind, you know where to find us."

"I do." Kade watched as she went inside the club to rejoin her friends.

His gums were aching, and his body starving, but he had a job to do, and eating was not on the agenda until the mission was complete.

A howl of triumph pierced the night, followed by faint screams not far away.

Dread washed over Kade.

He broke into a run, only slowing when he approached a single-story building with a sign that proclaimed it a community center.

A man burst out the doors and gazed around. His shirt was torn, and he had bite marks on his arm. Eyes wide with panic, he tried to utilize a device similar to the one the woman Kade had just met had been using.

"What happened?" Kade asked.

The man started to speak, stopped, and waved behind him with a shudder. "There—" He paused, then started again. "There's been an attack. P-people are hurt. I need to call 911." He dropped his device.

Kade picked it up and held on to it. "What kind of attack?"

"I-I don't know w-what they were, but there were two of them."

As shock set in, Kade had the man sit down on the steps and pulled his pack off his back. Then before the guy knew what was happening, he administered the antivenom. "You won't remember this," Kade murmured as he wiped the guy's mind and sent him home with the thought that he'd fallen and hit his head after a dog attacked him.

Once the man was gone, Kade crushed the cell phone, then tossed it in the trash bin at the doors—he didn't know if the guy had gotten any video footage, but if he had it wouldn't be good if he started to show it around. He hurried up the steps and entered the building, then sucked in a deep breath. About thirty humans, most under sixteen, had been bitten. The few adults, who were able to, tried to help and comfort the younger children who were all crying or writhing on the floor as the weren toxin took over.

But there were no dead.

Concerned over the fact that the weren seemed intent on turning humans rather than killing them, Kade steeled his heart against their pain and took control of the room with his mind. He quickly administered antivenom, though the use of his mental ability was a strain, and keeping his fangs from sinking into one of the humans who'd been hurt wasn't easy.

Rage seethed as he implanted the thoughts that it had been a rabid dog attack tonight before sending everyone home.

Though he needed to find his sister, Kade set out after the weren responsible for this latest attack. Despite his messing with their minds, he knew that the children, and possibly some of the adults, would be traumatized for life over what had been done to them.

Tense, hungry, and fueled by anger, Kade was even more careful to avoid humans where he could. He didn't want to become their worst nightmare since this evening would end up giving many humans horror-filled dreams for a very long time.

But as the scent trail started to peter out, Kade worried he'd lose it as well. This mission was turning into a real pain in his ass, kind of like his sister. Speaking of, when he caught up to her, there'd be hell to pay. He still couldn't believe she'd let the grem loose on his ship and taken off with one of his fighters. Why? It wasn't like she had a reason to come here, so why did she? Could her desire to meet a human be the reason? Though she did and could drink blood, she didn't need it to survive. Not like he did.

As he covered miles of ground, Kade realized that he might never know, even if he did catch up to her. He'd learned long ago that not much Indris did made sense to him. Besides, she didn't often see the need to explain herself, which never helped.

Kade stopped and took stock of his surroundings. He was in a seedier neighborhood. Even the shadows seemed filled with evil tonight. He liked to think it was the weren's fault, but the trail had just about gone cold.

About to give up and head back to see if he could pick up his sister's trail again, the rich aroma of human blood filled his nostrils.

Then he heard it. Sounds of humans being attacked and turned.

Kade let out a faint whistle in an attempt to draw out any weren that he could, then waited in the shadows beside a school. Within moments, one of the vile beasts rounded the corner and stopped. Half wolf and half human, he stood on two legs. With shaggy patches of black fur, and his face more wolf than human, his nose twitched. A light of familiarity for Kade's species filled his eyes. "Bloodsucking Andrican. What brings you to Earth? Come to play with your food, have you?"

"Didn't you get the notification? It's annihilate all fangy furballs night. Though the timing could have been better, you're disrupting my R&R, and I can't say I'm pleased about that."

The weren, an older male, opened his mouth in a grin, showing off his large canines that were glistening with blood and saliva. "Come get me then. I'd hate to keep you waiting."

He may have been an elder, but he wasn't an ancient, and Kade was in the mood to let off some steam. But after his enemy got in a lucky swipe with his claws, leaving deep grooves in Kade's chest, he drew his blaster. His fists, while strong, weren't a match for claws and fangs. Plus, Kade didn't have the time for this crap right now. He shot the creature and watched as it dissolved into a ball of energy, then dissipated.

He quickly rounded the school and took care of a second weren, administering more antivenom to the humans. Kade had just sent the frail Earthlings on their way when Mayara's voice came through his comm unit. "We have a problem, Cap."

"I noticed."

"Cap?" Mayara asked, confusion in his voice.

Kade sighed. "The weren are turning humans."

"What? Why would they do that?"

"When I find out, I'll let you know." It was odd. The weren were a very protective, insular race. It wasn't often that they brought an outsider into their packs. This meant they were careful not to randomly turn others, as they became responsible for them. And from what he understood, they often vetted any requests to be turned, as not all survived the transformation. "What have you got?"

"Well, this might be something. I found another weren ship," Mayara said. "A class five POS named *Harbinger*, and it's been damaged. I managed to bring up the flight log and it's been here approximately two months."

"That coincides with the *Dadeus* going dark," Kade said, wondering what it all meant.

"It does. I'm thinking this pile of junk got into it with the *Dadeus*, stranding it here," Mayara said. "You think they're trying to start a pack on Terra Nova?"

"Possibly." Likely. Kade swore.

"We can't chance the humans finding this. There's no life support left, but I've managed to rig it enough to get it out of here and set it to self-destruct once it's a good distance from the planet."

"Good thinking."

"Find your lovely sister yet?" Mayara asked.

"No, she's hidden her trail," Kade said, then checked in with the rest of his hunters.

They all responded except Viper.

"What the hell is going on here?" Kellan asked.

"Are all the weren you're hunting turning humans as well?" Kade asked.

His hunters replied in the affirmative.

Viper cut in. "I've got a school full of kids hit. The furballs broke up a dance. I'm going to need more antivenom and some help here."

"Since everyone's low on the stuff, I'll have Mayara send Nico down with more," Kade said.

"I'm close to you. I'll head over," Kellan told his brother.

"As am I," Antoli said.

Satisfied Viper had enough help headed his way, Kade contacted Mayara again. He'd just turned his comm unit to silence when a pained human scream split the night.

Kade darted in a blur across a busy intersection and into an even rougher residential neighborhood. The homes were tiny, and though some were taken care of, others were in various states of decline with yards overflowing with trash and weeds.

Still, the odd kid went door to door, a far cry from the numbers who'd been out in the nicer subdivisions he'd passed through earlier.

Kade let his instincts guide him, and within moments found himself across the street from a closed automotive shop.

"Run," a female voice shouted from somewhere behind the building.

A moment later, a young girl wearing fake cat ears and a long black tail raced past Kade. Tears streaked the black whiskers drawn on her face. *What the helltar?*

Blood, and not the sweet stuff he'd been smelling all evening, made Kade want to gag. It had a taint to it he'd only ever come across in the vilest beings.

Kade silently rounded the building and stared in shock at the scene in front of him.

A pack of snarling and growling weren fought a slender human. A female.

She was dressed in skintight black pants and a shirt, giving the beasts a run for their money.

The stench was overpowering.

Kade moved closer and spotted a weren lying motionless on the ground.

The tainted reek came from a dead human man lying in a puddle of noxious fluids that burned his sinuses.

The weren snarled as they circled the female.

"What are you nasty bastards waiting for?" she taunted them.

She was glorious. With long reddish-brown hair, her green eyes glinted as she wielded the blade in her hand like a pro.

As Kade blocked the disgusting smells, the female's scent hit him like a punch in the gut.

Amazing. Divine. Hunger rose, harder than it had all night. It roared within him, and his fangs punched through his gums. Then fury at the weren overtook him.

3

Hunting Predators

APOLLY DONNED HER WEAPONS, tied her long hair back, then slid her leather jacket on with barely a glance in the dresser mirror.

The worried, dark-green eyes of her nineteen-year-old sister, Alidonna, followed Apolly across the room to the door. "I wish you wouldn't go. I have a bad feeling about tonight."

"You always have a bad feeling. I'll be fine. You know I have to do this, and you know why." Apolly tucked her updated list of local sex offenders in her pocket, grateful for the internet. The destroyers of innocents would be out in force tonight, just waiting to lure a little boy or girl away. Her sister had been one of those children seven years ago, and Apolly couldn't stand to let another get hurt. Not if she could help it. As long as there was breath in her body, she'd fight.

And Halloween always brought more of the pervs out.

She hugged her sister, tucking a stray strand of dark hair

out of Ali's face. "Don't worry. I'll be back in a few hours. Go put on a funny movie and pop some popcorn, or eat some ice cream. I got your favorite."

"I'm connecting with some friends online to test out my new game," Ali said, hugging her back.

Apolly smiled. Of course, she was. "Okay, well, have fun then. And don't open the door to anyone."

Her sister rolled her eyes at something Apolly knew she wouldn't do. Alidonna had barely left the house since her abduction.

Anger surged at those who preyed on the innocent. Yet as Apolly wove her way through the neighborhood to the home of the first sex offender, she felt exhilarated being out at night. For some reason, she always had, much more than she enjoyed being out during the day.

Her sister called her weird. Apolly supposed she was right.

She quickly made her way to her first destination with no time to waste. Lights were on in the tidy little house and the television could be heard.

As much as she'd love to go in and slit the man's throat, it appeared that the guy's elderly parents were home as well.

Apolly watched for a few moments until she spotted the creepy, balding man in the window. She'd been keeping an eye on him for a year now, and so far, she hadn't caught him doing anything wrong. Which just irritated the crap out of her.

When she'd first started going after the child predators, the urge to kill every one of them drove her. So she set a code. Unless she saw them doing something—hurting someone— she'd leave them alone. Yet every time she recalled the horror her sister had suffered through, it took all her strength to keep to that code.

She went to the next address, which turned out to be

completely dark, as did the one after it. Shit. This wasn't good. If they weren't home, where were they? She shivered at the thought of what they might be doing.

As she made the rounds to the rest of them, Apolly kept her eyes on the children out trick-or-treating. They had no idea of the sick individuals in their midst.

At least the youngest were usually accompanied by their parents. But it was the teenagers that roamed alone that worried her.

She spotted a tall, skinny man hanging back a bit, trying to appear as if he were traveling with a group of kids and parents.

Apolly watched him while scanning all around constantly.

She tensed when a little girl with wings on her back came running up to the man and held her sack of candy out. "Daddy, it's too heavy. You carry it."

Apolly relaxed and continued past the group, eyes peeled.

Down the street, a man emerged from between two homes and followed a young boy. Apolly picked up her pace, watching, waiting for the moment he showed any sign of wrongdoing. A block later, he ducked inside a known crack house.

She kept going toward the next place on her list. But as she drew close to the seedy home, she shivered. Everything was too quiet. She glanced around but didn't notice anything out of the ordinary. Yet the shadows continued to close in around her.

With a mental shake, Apolly reprimanded herself for letting her mind wander, yet something was pulling her to the end of the street.

A sense of urgency had her running across a basketball court. Across the street was an old gas station turned automotive shop. A handful of cars littered the lot, but it was the fear-filled cry of a child behind the place that chilled her. Evil lurked close by.

Apolly quietly made her way around the building and pulled up short.

A young girl huddled against the wall while a—what in the demons of hell was that thing?

Sure, it was Halloween, but she didn't need the gifts she was born with to know this wasn't someone dressed up. It looked like a midnight black wolf, only much larger. And a hundred times scarier.

Large fangs dripped blood as silver, glowing eyes watched her.

Then she saw what was beyond the creature.

"Hey, he's all yours." Apolly raised her hands as she tried to wrap her mind around what she was seeing. The man lying in a puddle of blood and urine, with his throat ripped open, was Gerald Keener. Number four on her list.

Apolly slid her knife from its sheath and kept her eyes trained on the wolf-beast as she inched toward the shaking child, who'd dressed up as a black cat for the night. "Are you hurt?"

The wolf-beast continued to watch them.

"Are you hurt?" she asked the girl again.

"I ... that man ... he tried to—" Tears ran down her face, and Apolly noticed her black cat-print top was torn. "The wolf stopped him."

Could he have been trying to protect the child?

Apolly shivered as the presence of evil grew more potent, and out of the shadows emerged more creatures. Only these looked to be part human and part wolf, and they definitely had a sinister vibe to them.

Werewolves? Really? Though they looked nothing like the movies depicted them.

Apolly tucked the girl behind her and inched to the corner

of the building. "Run," she hissed. The child didn't move. "Run!" Apolly shoved the girl back toward the street, then turned to the six new monsters crept toward her.

One of the evil beings started to go after the girl.

"No! Leave. Her. Alone!" Apolly screamed. Fury thrummed through her, and to her utter shock, the fur-covered man-wolf turned back, a startled look in his eyes. Then he rejoined his pack that slowly converged on Apolly.

The black wolf-beast who'd killed Gerald inserted himself between her and the pack and let out a menacing growl. Apolly shivered, glad he wasn't facing her.

They leaped on him.

Amid snarls and grunts, fangs tore and sliced at each other.

Apolly started to inch along the side of the building until another of the monsters broke off and circled, ending her escape. With a grin, he began to stalk her, herding her back toward his pack. "You'll make a nice mate for all of us."

Mate? WTF? No f'ing way. "Over my dead body."

"I'd rather you be alive. But if that's what it takes, then so be it." The monster leered.

Apolly shuddered, then seeing no way out, she braced herself. "What are you nasty bastards waiting for?"

As the black wolf-beast fought off three of the werewolf creatures, the others dogged Apolly, and it wasn't long before she realized they were playing with her.

Determined to wipe the leers from their faces, Apolly used all the skills she'd learned over the last seven years. She managed to take one down and had another squealing from a cut of her blade, then claws raked her legs and knocked them out from under her.

Pain swept through her. Apolly ignored it and managed to

jump out of the way, but not before another grabbed her bicep in a pinching grip.

Apolly yanked her arm free and glanced over to see the monsters bring down the black wolf who'd tried to protect her. "Get away from him!"

One of them raised his claws to deliver a killing strike to the black wolf.

Rage at what was about to happen gave her strength. "I said. Get. Away. From. Him!" Apolly sank her dagger deep into the creature's back. As she yanked it free, the creepy werewolf let out a howl and turned on her.

Apolly stabbed him again, this time in the chest.

But he didn't go down.

He backed off and flashed a glance at the wolf. "I'll take care of you later," he told Gerald's killer. Then, with an evil grin, he joined his brethren, who were back to circling Apolly.

Throbbing agony radiated through her body as she attempted to back up again. It was going to take more than her blade to get out of this mess. At that knowledge, worry for her sister consumed her. How would Ali survive without her?

Not yet ready to give in, Apolly drew on the strength of her grandmother's bloodline and scrambled up onto an old airconditioner unit.

A set of extremely sharp canines pierced her ankle. Apolly kicked hard and fast, satisfied when the monster squealed.

"What, you thought I'd be easy prey? You might get me, but I promise to hurt you first, so bring it!" She was ready.

A shove from behind sent her flying.

Apolly hit the ground and rolled, coming to a stop as a big brute of a man joined the melee. With golden-blond hair and blue eyes, he wore a shredded black sleeveless shirt through which Apolly could see the glorious muscles of his chest.

She tore her gaze away and shook her head. Great, here she was fighting for her life, and all she could think of was some stranger's six-pack. Except, it wasn't just a six-pack but a very yummy-looking eight-pack. That wasn't all. The guy was corded with solid muscle from top to bottom. Yup, completely ripped.

The evil wolfy men had backed off, surprise evident in their eyes. "Andrican."

The gorgeous blond ignored them, instead turning a pair of stunning blue eyes on Apolly.

Her breath caught and her heart double-tapped.

His eyes gleamed appreciatively. "You fight well. Want some help?"

Yeah, please! Save me, Mr. Ripped-sexy-hunk-man. Take me away from these vile creatures.

Gah! What the hell was wrong with her? She never reacted to men this way. "I got this."

"I don't doubt it." The man grinned.

Apolly's blood roared in her ears as her hands grew damp, and as he faced the werewolves, Apolly swore she saw ivory fangs in his mouth. This was the freakiest Halloween ever.

"Weren bastards." He spat. "Thought I'd pop by and even the odds a bit."

His voice sent ripples of pleasure through Apolly, which was so not the time or place for such things.

No, now was her chance to go, get out of here. But even as she tried to flee, Apolly couldn't take her eyes off Mr. Ripped. She watched, awed at the speed in which he fought all the monsters at one time. Claws raked and swiped, and before long, the remains of his shirt were shredded until it barely hung off him.

Apolly swallowed, wanting to touch, taste, and run her

hands and tongue all over the guy. She shook her head as if trying to clear the cobwebs. What the hell was she thinking? This was nuts. The whole night needed a do-over. She should have listened to her sister and stayed home.

But no matter what, Apolly knew she could never have done it. There were too many children that might need help.

Apolly drew a deep breath and pushed her desire for her golden-haired savior from her mind. Now would be the time to skedaddle.

She couldn't move. Mr. Ripped moved like some kind of well-seasoned warrior, though Apolly had no idea where one would train for something like this.

The snarling monsters didn't stop their relentless onslaught.

Still, despite how hard they fought, her guy was clearly the better fighter. Wait, her guy?

As if they were suddenly tired of this, two of the creatures glanced at each other, then backed away. They watched for a moment longer, then glared over at Apolly. "We'll see you later." Then they turned and raced off.

Mr. Ripped growled and looked as if he wanted to follow them, but the rest of the beasts kept him occupied. He stepped up his pace, and within moments the ground was littered with ugly, patchy fur-covered monsters, some silent, others moaning.

As he snapped the neck of each creature and swirling light rose from the bodies, Apolly sucked in a breath. "What the hell?" She gazed around, but all signs of the evil freaks had vanished. "Impossible."

The black wolf-beast—Gerald's killer—tried to pull himself to his feet.

Mr. Ripped was on him, a fiery light in his blue eyes.

"No, don't," Apolly said. "He's not with the rest of them. He saved the girl and tried to keep the pack away from me."

"She's been bitten."

Apolly gaped at the wolf. "You can talk?" She'd heard the others speak as well, but then they appeared to be part human. The wolf-beast looked like a massive wolf. She turned to Mr. Ripped. "He spoke. He's a wolf, and he ..." She shook her head and closed her mouth.

Mr. Ripped didn't appear impressed. "You were bitten?" he asked her instead.

"What?" Apolly was starting to feel a little light-headed, but what could you expect after fighting monsters that shouldn't exist?

"I asked if you were bitten," the sexy hunk said.

Apolly shrugged. "I ... I don't know. I don't think so." She looked over her body, which was now screaming in pain. Both her shirt and pants were covered in blood and shredded. Ruined. "Maybe." Apolly's legs gave out. "Think I'll just sit for a minute. Catch my breath."

Mr. Ripped snarled and hurried over to her. "Where did they get you?"

Apolly could only look up at him. He was so yummy looking. "Ow!" she yelped when he stuck her with something. She glared at him and rubbed her arm. "What was that?"

"Antivenom."

Intense blue eyes that she swore were glowing, studied her.

"Anti ..." Apolly's heart fluttered.

"You're hurt."

"So are you." She stared at the gashes in his chest, then sucked in a deep breath as fiery agony suddenly engulfed her. She'd pushed the pain away while fighting, but now it was burning through her and quickly becoming unbearable.

Mr. Ripped reached out to help her up, but as soon as their hands touched, lightning—liquid pleasure—shot through her, driving the pain back.

Apolly gasped, and Mr. Ripped jerked his hand away, eyebrows pulling into a scowl.

Apolly cradled her hand to her chest as if she'd been burned.

Blue eyes filled with flames of hunger stared right into her.

Apolly swallowed. "Who—what are you?"

4

Human Bonbons

Kade's breath left him in a rush at the sensation still tingling in his hand and up his arm. It was impossible, but he'd actually *felt* her. For the first time in his life, he experienced the touch of another as more than just pain or a slight pressure. It was beyond amazing. Heat warmed him, and fire licked his insides in an unimaginable pleasurable fire. It stirred his hunger to a fever pitch. His teeth ached, and his cock stiffened, harder than ever before. Everything converged, leaving him almost shaking with a deep raw need. One he'd never in his life felt or expected.

It left him shaken. Exposed. Vulnerable.

He didn't do vulnerable. Not since he was a child, and his caretakers brutally taught him never to let anyone put him in such a position.

The human stared up at him, her stunning green eyes

searching for answers. The scent of her sweet blood leaking from her wounds made the beast inside him rise.

Kade caught movement from the corner of his eye. The black weren in full wolf form was trying to escape. How had he forgotten about his enemy like that?

And how had this slip of a human managed to prevent him from ripping the weren's head from his shoulders? Could she be a witch? Whatever it was, he wouldn't let it happen again.

He was on the weren and fully prepared to end the bastard's life when a blur shoved him back.

Kade snarled, ready to attack this new enemy until he caught an all too familiar scent.

Indris.

She crouched in front of him, ready to attack. Silver fire blazed from her eyes, and her fangs and claws were fully extended. "Leave him alone, Kade."

"Indris, I've been looking for you." He scowled. "You let the grem loose on my ship."

She didn't answer, and it didn't matter. "Out of my way, Indi, his pack killed one of my hunters. Let me do my job, and we can talk later." He tried to go around her.

She blocked him. "I'm not interested in talking later, Kadey, and no one on the *Raken Claw* killed any of your hunters. If you need someone to blame, it was the grem and no one else."

As he went to pick her up, so he could move her, she hissed and swiped at him. "I want you to leave him alone. For once, will you please do something I ask?"

"Indi, have you lost your mind?"

Her eyes changed from pleading to hard, cold, and unwavering.

The wolf moved up beside her. "I'll not let you fight my battles."

Her silver eyes softened, and her hand sank into his fur. Then she met Kade's gaze. "If you care for me at all, you'll not touch him."

"What is going on here, Indris?"

She nodded at the wolf. "Kade, this is Rafarious. Rafe. And he's my mate."

"But he's a weren." Kade blinked, shocked for the second time in just a few minutes. "No. This can't be. How, Indi?"

"He is weren, and I'm half. And Rafe is one of the good ones. The grem were paid to bring me to Rafe when you intercepted us."

"I—" Kade didn't like it. "This is crazy."

"Maybe so, but I love Rafe, and he loves me," she said.

"He may not have killed my hunter, but he's still a killer."

Indris scowled. "Really, we're going to go there? What about you? You and your hunters are killers as well, dear brother, so I don't think you should be pointing fingers at anyone."

"That's different. I don't hurt innocents," he snapped. He didn't want to kill his sister's mate in front of her eyes.

"Neither does Rafe or his pack."

As he stared at her in disbelief, she nodded. "But the other weren here do, and we must stop them."

"The ones from the *Harbinger*?" Kade asked.

"You know?" Indris asked, taken aback.

"We found their ship. It's them attempting to turn the humans?" Kade asked.

"They're starting a new pack," Rafe informed him.

Kade snorted. "Here on Earth, are they nuts? They'll be killed, each and every one of them, then their families and friends and anyone affiliated with them will also die."

"Yes," Rafe agreed. "Unless they build an army."

An army? Then it hit him. "They want Earth?"

Rafe nodded. "They do, and the only way to keep it, is to turn vast amounts of humans."

Kade groaned, it was a lot to wrap his head around and he didn't have time to figure it all out. He glared at his sister. "Why didn't you tell me?"

She glared right back at him. "You egotistical, controlling ass! I tried. You wouldn't listen."

Before Kade could respond, Rafe flew past him to the human female.

His! Rage gave Kade a speed he didn't know he had. He stood over the female who'd gotten him so twisted up only moments ago and cringed when she whimpered in pain. "Back off," he told the wolf. "Indris's mate or not, I won't let you hurt this one."

"The antivenom isn't working." The weren—Rafe, whoever the fuck he was—reached for the female on the ground.

A growl started deep in Kade's chest. "I said, back off."

Indris once again sank her hand into the wolf's pelt. He eased back, not taking his eyes off Kade.

"Rafe is right," Indris said to Kade in a gentler tone. "The antivenom isn't working on your female."

"She's not mine." Though against his will, Kade found his gaze once more drawn to the woman who'd elicited such a reaction in him. She sat shivering and sweating.

Like a child playing with fire that he knew would burn him, Kade wanted to touch her again. It was all sorts of stupid, but he wanted to feel her fingers on him, pull her into his arms despite the fact he was still trying to come to terms with what happened the last time he made contact with her.

"Kade." Once he looked up, Indris continued. "I know what it feels like. I can tell she's your mate."

Kade frowned. "No, she can't be my mate."

Kiss of Darkness

"Mate, what are you both going on about?" the human female asked, then gasped and clutched her stomach.

"Do you have more antivenom?" Indris asked.

"No, I—" Helltar! "I used my last shot on her."

"You need to get her to the *Sentinally* fast, then," Indris said.

"Wait, what's the sun ... tan ... ally?"

"*Sentinally*," Kade said, correcting her. "It's my ship."

"What? I'm not getting on a ship." The woman's teeth began to chatter.

"Rafe and I have to go stop the *Harbinger* pack," Indris said. "Take good care of this one, Kade."

Before he could say anything more, his sister and Rafe were gone.

"Dorothy's ready to go home now," the human said, voice sounding shaky.

"Your name is Dorothy?" Kade asked.

"What? No!" She rolled her eyes. "Haven't you ever watched *The Wizard of Oz*?"

"The Wizard of who?"

"Never mind." She waved her hand. "I just really need to go home."

"I have to get you to my ship," Kade said, then steeled himself. He reached out and helped her stand, and her touch ignited a slow burn inside him. A burn that made his insides twitch at her enticing scent.

"Thank you, but I'm not going anywhere with you." She moved away, breaking contact.

Cold and numbness invaded Kade, reminding him of his childhood lessons.

As she tried to walk, but stumbled, Kade slipped an arm around her waist. His pulse began to race at her proximity, and his fangs ached.

"Well, this Halloween sure sucked the big one," she said, then indicated the deep slices in his chest. "I see they got you as well."

"Those are from earlier. I'll heal."

"Earlier? How many—? Oh, never mind. What were those things anyway?" she asked as he helped her out to the street.

"Weren. Nasty creatures." And a couple had slipped away.

"What are you called?"

"Apolly. Name's Apolly, short for Apollamina." She gasped and stumbled. "My insides ... burning." She was beginning to slur. "Need a hospital."

"Humans can't help you, but I can."

"Humans? You're not human?" she asked.

"I'm Andrican."

"Right. Nice to meet you, Andrican."

Kade didn't correct her.

She leaned even more on him, her head against his chest. Silky hair tickled his skin, making him shiver and imagine more of her tickling him, sliding against him. Skin to skin. He bit back a groan.

She wrapped a hand around his hip. "I need to go."

"You're in no condition to go anywhere on your own," he said, savoring her against him.

"Have to. Ali will worry." She paused and let out a little laugh. "She's going to freak, seeing me like this."

Desire withered and horror filled Kade. "Who is Ali?"

"Sister. She's ... alone."

Goalendamn! The weren had Apolly's scent, and if he knew anything about them, they'd go after her family next. "Where do you live?"

No answer.

"Apolly."

Kiss of Darkness

"Wh ... at?"

"You need to stay awake." Kade tried to push the command, but his compulsion hit a solid wall and fell away. Who was this female, and how was she able to keep him out of her mind? "Tell me what your address is."

"Can't. I don't even know your name, for all I know, you might be a serial killer."

Kade blinked down at her. He saved her life, and she thought him a serial killer? "I'm Kade."

But she didn't seem to hear, or care. Kade took a deep breath and tried again to get into her mind. He needed to pluck out her address in order to get it to one of his hunters. He'd also have to set someone on the trail of the two weren who'd slipped through his grasp. He pushed hard.

"Stop that!" She slapped his chest where he'd been raked by the weren earlier.

Kade ignored the pain. "Apolly, you need to give me your address so I can send someone to protect your sister."

"Can't, that'll scare her." Her eyes fluttered.

"Apolly! Stay awake," he said. "I promise my men won't scare or harm your sister, but we can't leave her alone."

Her eyes opened. "Why?" Understanding dawned. "Those monsters, they'll go after her?"

"Yes, I'm afraid so."

Moisture pooled in her green depths. "I've got to get home."

"You need to be healed first, or you'll be a danger to your sister. Tell me your address, and I promise she'll be protected."

"Promise?"

"I do," he said.

Apolly mumbled something, then her eyes fluttered closed. "So tired. Everything ... hurts."

Kade tapped his ear-comm unit as he scooped her into his

arms, marveling at how little she weighed. He sucked in a breath as her warmth suffused him. His cock was a throbbing mass of steel. "Mayara, I need transport to the *Sentinally* now."

"What's happened, are you injured?" Mayara asked.

"I have a woman here. She was attacked by a pack of weren. I gave her the antivenom, but it's not working. I have to take her to the *Sentinally*, and I need you to send someone to her home." He repeated the address Apolly had given him. "There's another young woman, her sister Ali, and she's all alone. I fear the weren who got away will be heading to her home to exact their revenge on the sister."

Mayara was silent for a moment, and Kade knew he was just as stunned at the idea of bringing an Earthling aboard their spacecraft, then he reached out to Kade's other hunters, asking their whereabouts. Mayara sighed. "Since no one is near that address other than me, I'll go."

"That won't work," Kade said. "I need transport to the *Sentinally*."

"The ship Indris took is close to you," Mayara said. "I'll send it to you, it'll be there momentarily."

"Yes, fine. We'll be waiting." Kade tapped his comm unit off, unable to take his eyes from the delectable female in his arms. Her long reddish-brown hair had fallen loose from its binding, and her lashes rested against pale skin. Skin that he couldn't help but wonder what it would feel like to touch. Who was she? It was apparent she wasn't entirely human, but he'd never encountered one such as her before. Not even the woman from earlier had affected him so strongly.

The desire to taste Apolly was shoved aside as another more primal part hungered to bury himself deep within her body—to sample her in every way possible.

Though he couldn't see it, Kade could feel the energy as the cloaked ship Mayara sent to him landed a few feet away.

Kade drew on his mental abilities and willed the hatch open. Then with Apolly in his arms, he climbed inside the vessel. The ship was meant for one pilot, but Kade settled Apolly against his chest and quickly secured them, praying to a deity he no longer believed in that they wouldn't be too late. He didn't know why she caused such a reaction within him, but she had to live, there was no other option.

But as her decadent sweet scent enveloped Kade, he had to fight the urge to sink his teeth into the smooth expanse of her neck and discover what she tasted like.

He tore his gaze from her creamy skin and set course for the *Sentinally*.

5

Turn or Die

The Novarian female, Belsuma, waited for him in the landing bay. "Mayara said you were bringing a human on board infected with weren toxin and that the antivenom didn't work."

"Yes," he replied, worry zinging through him. Apolly's pulse was beating much slower than it should.

"We can try another, but if that fails ..." Bel didn't finish the sentence and instead injected Apolly with another dose of antivenom. "It's done. It should kick in quickly if it's going to work. Take her to the infirmary so we can disinfect those wounds and close them."

In the med bay, Kade gently set Apolly on a bed.

Between him and Belsuma, they removed Apolly's clothing to make sure she didn't have any other bites or wounds, then waited as the med bed did its job of healing her. Then Bel frowned at him. "You're hurt."

"I'll heal." Though he should have done so already, and Bel knew it.

"You didn't feed. Why didn't you feed?"

"There wasn't any time." Besides, he sure wasn't going to break his own rule about feeding until they were done tracking the weren.

Bel sighed loudly. "You need to feed to heal."

Kade remained silent, studying Apolly. She was the most beautiful woman he'd ever seen, and he'd seen a lot of different females. Now, if she'd just open her eyes.

"She should be awake now," Bel said, gaze narrowed on Apolly. "But her skin's losing color and her pulse is beating much slower."

"What can we do?" Kade hated the fear in his voice.

Bel scanned her vitals again. "The second shot isn't working. She's dying."

"She can't. There has to be something we can do."

Bel paused, then nodded. "Blood. She needs blood to counteract the weren toxin. Your blood. Novarian won't work."

"You want me to turn her?"

"If you don't want her to die or end up a weren, then yes," Bel replied.

Apolly was a stranger, yet for some unknown reason, Kade couldn't stand the thought of her dying or turning into something he'd have to hunt down and kill. "She's a human." And as such, turning her was forbidden.

"I won't tell if you don't," Bel said.

There'd be hell to pay if the emperor ever found out. Not that he truly cared. And while he didn't usually trust most Novarians, of the three he had on board, he had to admit, he liked and trusted Bel the most.

Kade turned his gaze back on Apolly. She was amazing. A

fighter, and his reaction to her was beyond anything he could ever have imagined. Could she be his mate? The thought was alluring, yet frightening at the same time.

"Kade!"

He frowned at Bel. "What?"

"You know what. She doesn't have a lot of time left. You need to give her your blood, or she won't make it." Bel stared hard at him.

Kade's pulse kicked up a notch at the thought of what would happen when he did. Hunger surged the likes of which he'd never experienced. But no matter how much he might like the idea, once Apolly took his blood, it would change her. As newly turned, she'd lust for the crimson liquid. But she wouldn't have the control a natural-born Andrican did. She'd forever need blood, yet only his would nourish her. She'd also become immortal like him. But it was something else that had the monster inside him roaring.

Bel's eyes grew wide, then she grinned. "Don't wait too long."

As she left the infirmary, Kade swore and raked a hand through his hair. He should be down on Earth helping his hunters eliminate the weren. Not up here thinking of sinking deep into the body of the female dying in front of him.

Look at what she was already doing to him, how much worse would it get if she were turned?

Apolly moaned, and Kade knew he had no choice. He scooped her up in his arms, and they were almost to his quarters when she opened her eyes. "Kade?"

"You heard when I gave you my name?"

"Yes. Where are we going?"

"To make you feel better."

"Ali—" Panic filled her eyes.

"She's fine. I sent one of my men to keep an eye on her," Kade said, trying to ease her.

"No! She's terrified of men!"

"I'll let Mayara know, don't worry. He'd never harm her."

"He better not," Apolly muttered, then closed her eyes until he entered his quarters. They flipped open as the door slid shut behind them and Kade gently laid her on his bed.

Wary green eyes watched as he tapped his ear-comm unit. "Mayara, you locate the house yet?"

"I did. All is quiet here."

"Good, let's hope I'm wrong and it stays that way. The female inside is scared of men," Kade informed him.

"Got it. I won't even bother her unless I have to," Mayara said.

"Thanks, Mayara." Kade tapped his comm off, his body tensing under Apolly's gaze. Even on the brink of death, she was utterly lovely. Her scent wrapped him in a haze of need, and it was all he could do not to jump on top of her. As the one always in control, it was ironic that he was barely hanging on by a thread.

"What happened? How'd I get here?" Apolly gazed around, eyes widening as she caught a glimpse out the window. She struggled to sit up and fell back. "Where are we?"

"On my ship, the *Sentinally*. The weren infected you. We gave you more antivenom, but your body's rejecting it. We also disinfected and closed your wounds," he explained.

"Ship? Right, you did mention a ship, though silly me, I assumed you meant the kind that floats on the water."

"Nope, the kind that travels through space."

"This is impossible. I've got to be dreaming."

"It's no dream." It wasn't what he should be saying. He should agree with her, then wipe her mind. But he couldn't do it.

"You mean to tell me we're ... in s-space?"

"Right above Earth," he answered.

"That's bat-crap crazy, and who's *we*?" she asked.

"Bel, she's a medic and one of my pilots," he said.

"Ah-huh, sure ... and this all makes perfect sense. Not!" Apolly's hand slid over the thin sheet covering her. "Look, I appreciate you trying to help, but I've got to get home. Where's my clothing? My knife?"

"Your injuries needed tending. We had to remove them to fix you up. All your belongings will be returned to you." Kade sat on the edge of the bed.

Apolly tensed, then winced and grew even paler.

Kade's heart skipped a beat in fear for her. "You don't need to be afraid of me." At least he hoped that was the case. The way he was reacting to her wasn't something he had any experience with. "I won't hurt you, but I do need to explain some things."

Apolly waited.

Kade drew in a deep breath. "You were bitten. We gave you the antivenom, yet for some reason it's not working. We think your body is fighting the weren toxin on its own, but it's losing the battle."

Alarm spread across her face. "What does that mean? Am I going to change into one of those monsters?"

Kade swallowed. "We're trying to prevent that."

Apolly studied him. "I'm dying. I see it in your eyes. I'm right, aren't I?"

Kade nodded, a deep sadness welling up inside of him. "If

you let me, I can ensure that neither of those scenarios happen."

"I sense there's more to it."

"There is," he said. "You need to take my blood."

6

Consequences

"Like a transfusion?" she asked, her eyes narrowing on him. "But you're not human. How does that work?"

"Something like that, and therein lies the problem."

Apolly stared at him. Was he for real? Was any of this? How could she be floating above Earth in a spaceship? And Kade—who was injured himself, by the way—wanted to give her his blood? This was miles beyond nutso. Had the weren bite induced some kind of hallucinogen? That was it—she was out of her ever-loving mind.

Except, she was going on the idea that werewolves were real, which didn't make much sense either. Maybe she'd fallen asleep and only dreamed she went out tonight.

Her stomach cramped, telling her it was all real.

Nausea churned inside her.

Apolly tried to sit up again. Nothing happened. Her body wasn't working. "I ... don't feel well."

He nodded. "It's the weren toxin taking over. Once my blood is in your system, it'll eradicate it, and you'll begin to feel better almost immediately. Stronger."

"I don't want to die, or become like those evil creatures, so hook me up." Apolly grimaced as pain ripped through her. "Quick, I need to get home."

Kade shook his head. "I can't just hook you up. It doesn't work that way, and you need to be aware of a few things first."

"What, I'll turn into a ... frog?"

"A frog?" Kade blinked. "No, nothing quite so cute. I'm afraid you'll become like me, though."

"Like you. What exactly is that?" The pain made it hard to think properly.

"I am Andrican."

"I remember, but that doesn't tell me much." Apolly moaned as her skull felt like it were about to explode.

"Andricans are what you humans would call a vampire."

"Wh ... at?" Apolly gaped at him. "No bleeping way." She wanted to pinch herself but couldn't even do that. "I need to wake up now."

"This is the only way to stop you from turning weren, and to keep you alive. But if we do this, you'll be tied to me for the rest of your life," Kade explained.

Apolly could feel her body fighting, changing, and her heart beat so slowly. "And what? I'll grow fangs? Become some crazed, evil bloodsucker?" She shook her head, or at least she thought she did. "No, no way."

"We are not crazed, nor evil. Though you will crave blood, and find humans extremely hard to resist." He let her digest that.

"So, you're saying I'll want to eat everyone I meet?" she asked.

"Not eat, but you will want to drink from them."

"M-my s-sister?"

"Yes."

"No, I don't want that. There's got to be another way." Apolly wasn't one to cry at any little thing, but as the agony continued, she thought of her sister. Moisture pricked the backs of her eyes. "Ali depends on me."

"Then you'll have to be well-fed before you see her. If there were any other way, I'd do it. This is the only option to keep you alive and from turning weren that I know of," Kade said gently.

"And I'll need your blood to survive?"

"Yes," he answered.

Apolly blew out a breath. "Will you help me? Keep me from going around killing people?"

"Andricans don't go around killing people, but to answer your question, yes, I will." He hesitated. "There's one more thing."

"Of course there is."

"You won't be able to tolerate the light from any sun," he said.

Any sun? It took a moment for her to understand. "Really, I can't go out during the day?"

He shook his head, eyes sad.

Apolly thought about it. She never cared about basking in the sun and tanning like some of her friends used to. And when she did go out on a sunny day, she wore a hat or sat in the shade. It sucked, but if it was death or the sun, what choice did she have? Plus, she worked from home as an editor and was more of a night person anyway. "Well, that's going to take some adjusting, but ... okay. Let's do it."

"Are you sure? As I said, this will tie us together forever. You'll be dependent on me for blood. I also have to warn you that I want you, and drinking blood can be very sexual."

The very thought of consuming his blood should've made Apolly cringe, but for some reason it didn't. As for the sexual part, well, she'd never met anyone who affected her the way Kade did. In fact, she had been starting to question if there was something wrong with her since none of the men she met even tempted her.

Until she laid eyes on Kade. He was one super-sexy man—scratch that, vampire, and she was attracted to him in a way that was almost scary.

"You're hurt." She stared at his chest. "You should get that taken care of."

"It's fine. I'll heal."

Could she really do this? Because as it was, she was craving this strange vampire in ways that shocked her. And somehow, she knew that drinking his blood would send that craving into a realm all its own.

Apolly felt her face heating and glanced out the window. "How will this work with me down there on Earth and you up here?"

"We'll figure it out," he said, voice serious. "I need to drain most of your blood from you first."

"How?" she asked, though she knew.

"I have to drink from you." His eyes began to glow.

A shiver of pleasure shot through her. "If I'm infected, won't you get infected?"

"No, weren toxin doesn't affect my kind," he said.

"Will it hurt?"

"No," he answered, though there was a hungry light in his eyes.

"Right." Apolly's breath hitched and she tilted her neck to give him access.

"You'll become very weak, don't fight it," he said.

Kade slid his arm around her and pulled Apolly close. He was wonderfully warm and hard, so very *hard*. The ache to run her hands all over his ripped body had her doing just that as he sank his fangs into her neck.

Apolly's body began to throb. He'd said pleasurable, but nothing prepared her for this. She couldn't stop touching him, wanting him in a way she never imagined she could want anyone. This intensity was the stuff of movies and books, not real life.

Kade pressed closer and made a whimpering sound. He was trembling as well.

Apolly savored the feel of his skin, his hard body, and slid her hands down his pants to his ass.

But then her mind started to grow foggy, and it grew harder to draw breath. She began to panic.

Easy, sweet Apolly, easy now. Just a bit more, then you will feel better, Kade said, his words a caress of her mind as his fangs withdrew. He backed off, and Apolly felt something at her lips. *Drink.*

She should have questioned how she could hear him, but instead her lips opened, and the first drop of blood hit her tongue. It sizzled, rich and intoxicating.

"That's it," Kade crooned, a slight tremble to his voice as he cradled her close. His fingers stroked her hair gently. "Keep drinking."

Apolly did, and suddenly her heart was beating out of control. She opened her eyes and lost herself in Kade's blue eyes. Hunger, heat, and desire shone in the glowing depths that seemed to stare straight into her. Something awoke in Apolly.

Kiss of Darkness

She lowered her lips to his wrist, and as his blood entered her system, she began to tingle all over.

He tasted sweet, heady, like a fine liquor. With his blood came an intense energy. Power. It rocked Apolly and tore a ragged moan from her throat. Or was that his throat? She was no longer sure.

All she knew was she needed more. Apolly burrowed in closer to him.

Kade's breathing sped up.

Apolly held his glowing gaze, aware of what was happening to him. He wanted her. Wanted to consume her. To fuck her, and badly.

That normally would have sent her racing away, but her body was also burning for him.

He was a magnificent male. What would he look—feel—like naked? The rigid member pressing against her was rock solid, and Apolly swore it was pulsing, though she didn't think men's penises did that, at least not to her knowledge. But then, her experience was pretty limited.

And Kade wasn't human. At that thought, fire swirled low in her belly and between her legs. What would sex with a vampire —Kade—be like? She couldn't imagine it wouldn't be anything short of amazing.

Suddenly a very vivid image filled her mind, one of him rising above her, then sinking between her legs, pushing deep and filling her up. His eyes would hold her captive as he began to move. His hips and ass muscles would flex as he pumped hard and faster into her.

"Oh, beautiful goddess, Apolly," Kade whispered, her name shivering through Apolly.

Somehow, she had projected her vision to him.

She should have been horrified but couldn't summon the

emotion—she wanted him too badly, and the connection they seemed to be sharing was incredible. Amazing. Through it she could feel her desire, her hunger, along with his. Kade wanted her. More than that, he wanted to consume her, taste her, take her, and hear her scream his name. She felt his struggle to hold it all at bay and not give in.

Brilliant blue eyes seared straight into her soul. "I didn't know it would be like this," he whispered, cradling her with tenderness.

Apolly continued to burn, but in a pleasurable way and not in agony. Kade's blood was potent, and she could feel new strength traveling through her veins. With it came an insatiable hunger for more. She began to writhe against him, unable to get enough. She wanted it all. Him, his blood, everything.

Something inside shattered, a surrender, and Apolly took Kade's other hand and slid it up under her shirt, needing to feel his touch.

With a groan, Kade pulled her onto his lap, his steel rod pressing against her. Apolly shuddered as his hand seared the skin of her breast. *You're so soft. I want to touch all of you.*

You're in my head again, she said and felt his shock.

You heard me?

I did. I thought it was intentional, she said.

His voice—his presence, a strange yet welcome connection, sent giant flames of wildfire licking through Apolly. *I want you to touch me, Kade.* She arched against him. *I want to feel you inside me.* She burned, ached, needed, and hungered.

Kade's eyes reflected the same things back at her, straight to her soul. *Are you sure? Because I want you so badly that if we start this, I'll be unable to stop.*

Yes. Please, I'm on fire. And she was. Heat was burning and whipping through her veins.

Kade groaned, and in a blink, they were both naked. "You've had enough for now. Lick my wrist to close it."

Apolly didn't want to stop drinking the nectar of his blood, but she wanted him inside her more. She licked his wrist and watched as the two spots closed immediately. Kade shuddered hard.

Apolly held his gaze and licked his wrist again.

Kade sucked in a deep breath, and his fangs flashed.

Warmth pooled between Apolly's legs, and her heart thundered as their connection, combined with the fire in Kade's blue eyes, conveyed what she was doing to him.

With a smile, Apolly slowly licked her bottom lip, then wrapped her hands in his hair and pulled his head down to her.

7

Hungry Vampire

KADE'S BREATH exploded in a rush, and he rose over Apolly. Never had he ever dreamed that a simple touch, or lick, could cause anything but pain. Turned inside out, Kade was completely on fire. His blood raged, and his gums ached with his desire to sink once more into the smooth, tender skin of Apolly's neck. She was life, the best thing he'd ever tasted, and he needed more. He needed her blood and body—to sink deep within her heat and take her in ways he never dreamed.

The imagery she'd shared with him earlier had stunned Kade and left him fighting with the desire to do exactly what she'd shown him. And more. So very much more.

As she took his blood, her hands seared him, and he was a bundle of energy and nerves, craving more and unable to get enough. He ached to touch her plump, creamy breasts, to feel her, lick her as she had him.

He had no idea how this would work; she was a human from Earth, technically off-limits, and he had a ship to captain.

Yet there was no going back, and as Apolly's fingers raked through his hair, then pulled his lips to hers, Kade let it all go. He couldn't have resisted if he wanted.

His body was no longer his now but belonged to the one beneath him.

No female had ever caused him to lose control to the extent he couldn't keep his fangs retracted. But Apolly wasn't just any female.

As their lips touched, Kade sighed inwardly. Yes, this was what he'd been missing all his life, and he'd never even known it. Apolly felt soft, yet strong, and tasted divine. He couldn't get enough of her. Kade's hands roamed over her smooth skin as he deepened the kiss.

Apolly's tongue met his, exploring, tasting him back. She moaned, then she stroked his fangs.

Kade shuddered as she caressed one, then another.

Then Apolly projected what she was about to do, and Kade groaned as she purposely pricked her tongue on the tip of one fang. Her blood roared in his head.

Kade held himself impossibly still as her decadent blood merged with his.

Beyond sweet, she was light, heaven, and the sun, all mixed together. The beast within Kade screamed for more. He wanted all of her, ached to claim her, take her, own her until Apolly belonged to him, heart and soul. The impulse was so demanding that the beast within him snarled.

He pulled away as the roaring in his head grew louder.

Apolly's green eyes held him immobile while her hands singed his skin as she drew them up his sides. Trails of fire followed—skin tingling and warm.

Then she reached for his throbbing cock. Kade shut his eyes and fought not to move as she stroked him.

"I want you deep inside of me, Kade." Her whispered words unraveled all control, and his cock began to weep.

He could barely talk as he struggled to hold off the beast that wanted to dive into her, to plunge deep without care and take everything. But he feared scaring her, or worse, hurting her.

"Do you want me, Kade?" she asked.

"I ... yes. So badly."

Yet somehow, he held still as Apolly pleasured him in a way he didn't even know possible. Her touch was the magic that ignited him as she stroked and cupped him, her tongue teasing his mouth, ear, and neck. Baby fangs raked his shin.

Sex had always been an impersonal outlet to shed energy, nothing else. He had a feeling Apolly would show him what the Novarians meant.

"I feel it in you. I feel your struggle, your control. I know you won't hurt me," she said.

How? How did she know that when he didn't? The beast was thundering inside him, threatening, demanding. His blood was on fire, his body aching, throbbing, pulsing.

"If you don't take me now, I'll erupt in flames." Apolly released his cock and pulled him down on top of her, arms holding him close.

His greedy, pulsing shaft nestled between her legs, the thick head pressing impatiently at her moist entrance.

Kade groaned, heart racing out of control.

Apolly gripped his ass, and her heat sent little flickering tongues of flame through every inch of Kade. Her body was everything he never knew he needed or wanted.

His lips sought hers once again, and unable to hold back,

his tongue plunged inside her, knowing he'd never get enough. She was the fuse to his spark.

Apolly wrapped her legs around his waist, opening herself to him. *I don't want gentle. I'm on fire.* She thrust images at Kade depicting him buried balls-deep inside her. *I want you. All of you. Now, Kade.*

A growl burst from his throat, and he released her mouth, fighting for control as he slid slowly between her folds. Exquisite pleasure shuddered through him, building to a fever pitch.

Apolly's sheath clenched around him tight. Holding him, squeezing him, as he inched farther into her heated depths.

"Oh God, Kade. Yes!" Apolly began to pant. Kade wrapped his arms around her, holding on, holding her still, holding back as much as possible. The beast thundered as he slid into her.

"Apolly!" Overwhelmed, Kade once again claimed her mouth, drawing Apolly's breath into his lungs. He teased her sharp little fangs like she did to him earlier.

I have fangs. Surprise registered through their connection, then pleasure. *I want to taste you again, Kade.*

I am all yours. He gripped her tighter.

Quit holding back! Needle-sharp fangs sank into his shoulder.

The bite sent endorphins flooding his system—a pleasure that stunned Kade with its intensity. He roared and pulled out only to thrust back in, hard, deep, then again.

Yes, Kade, don't stop. This is so much better than chocolate! Apolly cried, and any walls she'd had in her mind dissolved.

All of a sudden, Kade could feel what his blood was doing to her.

Apolly clung to him, withdrew her fangs, and licked the

twin punctures closed. Then she tilted her head, exposing her neck. "Now your turn. I want to feel all of you in me."

Kade didn't question or think. He just acted. His fangs pierced her deep. With a cry, Apolly shuddered beneath him.

Sweet, rich blood filled him in a way none ever had, and he knew that no matter who he drank from, none would taste as good, or fulfill him in the same way as Apolly's did. She was his other half, his soulmate.

It was more than he could stand. The dam burst, and his control unraveled. He withdrew his fangs, licked the creamy expanse of her neck, then found one soft creamy breast and sank his fangs deep again.

Apolly gasped, her fingers in his hair, holding him close as he drank the most exquisite blood he'd ever tasted.

His hips moved faster as her blood lit his on fire.

Apolly cried out and arched against him, her fingers clutching—digging into his back as her orgasm exploded through her. Kade felt the shock waves as they vibrated through him.

Apolly clenched tight around Kade's cock.

A fierce tingle traveled down his back and up from his toes, drawing his balls tight against him as he plunged harder and deeper than before, the monster inside taking complete control.

Body and soul on fire, Kade cried out as he exploded over the edge. But he couldn't stop. He never wanted to stop, and as the fierce need built once again, driving him higher, Apolly hung on.

Her little whimpers drove him onward. Harder, faster. He withdrew his fangs, lifted her legs, and drove himself in even deeper. He came hard a second time, body convulsing with shocking intensity. But he couldn't stop, and as his seed continued to spill into her, Kade collapsed. His cock throbbed and pulsed as if it would never end. Apolly held him close and Kade buried his face in her neck.

What they'd done had been amazing, but more than that, the arms holding him close made Kade realize what he'd been missing. No one had ever held him like he mattered.

But Apolly did, as if she never wanted to let him go.

A moment later, hunger rose up again and as soon as he stopped coming, he flipped Apolly over and drew her to her knees. Then like a being possessed, he drove into her from behind, groaning at how incredibly tight she was. Apolly began to pant, then she reached under and grabbed his balls. Her fingers were like heated brands caressing the most tender of places. Pleasure whipped through Kade and he began to quiver as she fondled and played with him.

"Harder," she said.

Kade held her breasts and plunged deep into her until they were both sweating and panting, then Apolly sent him an image.

Kade groaned and let her go. Apolly knelt in front of him and took him deep into her mouth.

She was careful of her new fangs as she showed him just how good it could be.

8

Missing

AFTERWARD, they lay in each other's arms.

"I never knew it could be like that." Apolly snuggled into him while her fingers traced designs on his healed chest.

"Neither did I," he said.

Apolly pulled back to look up at him, disbelief in her eyes.

Kade's face heated for the first time in his life. "It's true."

"I would say I find that hard to believe, but I know you're telling the truth." Apolly smiled.

Kade felt as if the light and heat from one of the universe's many suns, something no Andrican could tolerate, was shining upon his soul.

"Who was that woman earlier, with the wolf?" Apolly asked.

Kade didn't know what to think of his sister and what she'd

told him. "She's my sister, her name is Indris, and she's always been a handful."

"Well, she's very beautiful," Apolly said.

"Not as beautiful as you," Kade said, running his fingers over her soft skin.

Apolly ducked her head, but Kade could feel his words both embarrassed and pleased her.

"You are gorgeous as well. Are all Andricans good looking?"

"A lot are," Kade answered.

Apolly leaned over and kissed him, then stretched.

Kade felt himself growing hard again.

"I feel so good, like I could run a marathon." Then Apolly sat right up. "Holy crapoli, what time is it? I need to get back to my sister." She looked around his room. "I need my clothes, Kade."

Though he also felt amazing and wanted nothing more than to stay in bed and explore every inch of Apolly's body, the mention of her sister had him up and dressing. His hunters should have checked in.

He called Belsuma first. "Can you bring Apolly her clothing?"

"You were a little busy, so I left them outside your door," Bel said, and Kade could hear the grin in her voice.

Kade collected the bundle and handed it to the woman he had just spent the best moments of his life with. A woman he knew he'd not be able to let go.

As Apolly dressed, Kade contacted his crew on Earth.

All but Viper and Mayara responded. Kade glanced at Apolly, not wanting to worry her. "Mayara, check in."

No response.

He tried his surly warrior next. "Viper?"

Nothing.

"Kellan, how long since you saw your brother?" Kade asked.

"We parted ways after the mess at the school. He said he was on his way to help Mayara out," Kellan said. "Why?"

"He's not responding, and neither is Mayara," Kade said.

"That's not like him," Kellan said and Kade agreed.

"Cherro, Antoli, Rossa, any of you hear from either Viper or Mayara?" Kade asked.

None had.

Apolly stood at his shoulder, and despite his best effort to keep calm, he could feel the worry vibrate through her. Kade gave his hunters her address. "Each of you head over and find out what's happening. I'll be back down with you in just a bit." Kade glanced at Apolly and noted the determination in her eyes to go with him. "There's a young woman at the address who is scared of men, so use caution."

"Will do," Rossa said, and the others agreed.

Kade internally swore, not liking that two of his hunters were out of touch.

"I'm coming with you." Apolly raised an eyebrow daring him to say no.

Kade shook his head. "Remember what I told you about craving blood? It's not a good idea for you to come with me. It's too soon. You're newly turned and won't be able to shut down the craving. I'll go and I promise to keep you informed of what's happening."

Apolly moved in front of him and put her hands on her hips. "You are not leaving me up here."

"You'll be a liability down there," he said. "Besides, there won't be a lot of time. It's still night, but the sun will rise before long and we can't be out in it."

Her jaw firmed. "I don't care. My sister is in danger. Because

Kiss of Darkness

of me. If it were your sister, would you sit back and let others go?"

Kade knew he wouldn't. "Fine, but you stick close to me so I can help if you get the urge to taste someone."

Though her eyes widened, she nodded. "I will."

As much as he preferred the one-seater and Apolly on his lap, he didn't need the distraction. He picked a two-seater. He waited until his mate was settled in before lowering himself into his own seat. And though she was worried about her sister, the light in Apolly's eyes as she demanded he teach her how to turn on and control the ship made him smile.

He dreaded what they might find down on Earth, and the time getting there went by much too fast. Kade found a secluded spot in a park close to where Apolly lived and landed, activating the ship's cloaking system.

"Aren't you worried someone will find it?" Apolly asked after they climbed out.

"No, it's cloaked." Kade pointed behind them at the ship, and most of the human trick-or-treaters had retired for the night, which also helped matters.

"Oh, that's supercool, and"—Apolly shivered and gazed around—"dangerous if anyone found it. Do you know what they'd do to you and your crew if this was discovered?"

"I have an idea," Kade said, then tried to reach Mayara and Viper again to no avail.

Then he tried Kellan. "Where are you? You hear from your brother yet?"

"I'm still a good distance away and no," came the ominous reply.

Rossa buzzed him. "Cap, it's not looking good at the address you gave us. The door is busted open, and there's blood."

Dungshit! "Come on." Kade went to take Apolly's hand, but instead, had to put on a burst of speed just to catch up to her.

"I'm really fast now." Apolly grinned at him. "And I can see in the dark as if it were daylight."

He nodded. "I think you'll find there are many things you can do now that you couldn't before."

They arrived at her home within seconds and the sight of Kade's hunters gave Apolly a moment's pause. Then she was inside, shouting for her sister.

Silence met her call.

Kade ignored the stares of surprise from his crew and followed her in. Her small home looked like a whirlwind had swept through it. Apolly disappeared down a hallway, calling her sister's name.

Kade inhaled the different smells. The two weren that escaped them earlier in the night had been here, along with another four, one of which seemed faintly familiar. Though why that would be, Kade had no idea. But underneath the scent of weren was another. Blood, and not of the rich human variety either.

It was Andrican.

"Where is she?" Apolly returned, face pale. "Where's my sister?"

Kade wanted to pull her close and offer comfort, but from the anger vibrating within her, he didn't think she'd appreciate it. "We'll find them, I promise."

Rossa walked in and glanced at Apolly briefly before addressing Kade. "The blood is Mayara's." He held up a broken comm unit. "And Cherro found this."

"Goalendamn," Kade swore. They could heal from a lot of injuries, but not all, and judging by the scent—the amount of blood lost—Mayara had more than a scratch. "We need to find them now."

"Antoli and Cherro are tracking them as we speak," Rossa informed him.

Kade looked at Apolly. "Ready to go hunting?"

Without a word, she walked back outside.

A block away they found the imprint of what looked like a fight. The scent of weren was strong, leading Kade to believe Mayara had taken at least one out. But from the scuff marks and crimson on the ground, it was obvious Kade's main pilot, and possibly Apolly's sister, were both hurt.

Apolly's fangs lowered. "Ali's hurt. Wait. I can *smell* my sister. How is it I know this is hers from the smell?" She moaned and drew in a deep breath, then let it out. "And you're right, it's so sweet." She wrinkled her nose in disgust, and Kade knew through their connection it was toward her sudden craving.

Antoli's voice came through Kade's comm. "Cap, we found Mayara and the girl."

"Where?" Kade asked.

"At the shuttle." Antoli hesitated.

Cherro piped up. "There's more ..."

"What?" Kade asked.

"I think you should get over here, and make it fast, Captain." Antoli gave him the coordinates of where Mayara had hidden the spacecraft.

Kade looked at Apolly. "Your sister's with Mayara at the shuttle."

Kade contacted Kellan next. "Anything on your brother yet?"

"No."

Kade gave him directions to the shuttle. "Meet us there."

They ran—fast—up and down hills and around clumps of dried trees and brush, but as they came around a bend in the trail, Kade stopped short and silently swore.

Apolly stopped beside him, eyes riveted ahead. "What is this? Who are they?"

A group of fifteen weren huddled in front of the shuttle, while Cherro and Antoli stood just inside the open door, blasters in their hands.

9

Truth and Courage

KADE WAS FULLY PREPARED to fight his way through the pack, until he spotted his sister at the front of the group. A large, dark-haired male stood beside her, obviously Rafe in human form.

The weren parted to let them pass.

Skin prickling, Kade kept Apolly between him and Rossa. "What's going on, Indi?"

On the ground in front of his sister and her mate lay an injured weren. Though he hadn't fought Apolly earlier in the evening, Kade knew from his scent that he was part of the group who'd ransacked her home and attacked Mayara and Ali.

His faintly familiar stench curdled Kade's stomach. He studied the weren in his blotchy, ash-furred half-form. As he met the beast's red, anger-filled eyes, Kade frowned. He knew the male, but from where?

Despite his sister being at the head of the small group, Kade was happy to see Cherro and Antoli hadn't lowered their weapons. Though he did ignore the question in both their gazes regarding Indris with their enemy.

"We caught this ... *monster* stalking Mayara and the female." Indris sneered at the weren on the ground, then looked at Kade, a light in her eyes that he didn't quite understand.

"Where's Mayara? Ali?" Kade asked his hunters.

"Inside." Cherro nodded behind him. "Mayara's hurt badly, and the girl won't let us near him."

"What?" Apolly went to pass them, but Cherro stopped her. "I think you need to wait."

"Don't go anywhere," Kade told his sister, then led Apolly into the shuttle.

"S-stop r-right t-there," a terrified voice said from behind an open case of weapons.

Apolly gasped. "Ali, hon, it's me."

"Polly?"

"Yeah, baby, it's me." Apolly started for her sister, then stopped. Her whole body stiffened and Kade knew she'd caught the scent of fresh blood.

He was right beside her. "I feel your hunger." He laid a hand on her shoulder. "Easy."

Ali, who'd been holding a blaster she must've grabbed from the weapons stash—one capable of disseminating a large ship—started to lower the muzzle at the sight of her sister, but when she saw Kade, she raised it again and centered it on his chest. "P-polly, who's he?"

"It's okay, Ali. This is Kade. He won't hurt you, I promise," Apolly said.

"I saw something creeping in the shadows on my monitor, then these freaks from a bad horror movie broke into our home." Tears rolled down her cheeks. "I thought they were going to kill me."

Apolly nudged the weapon aside, then crouched down and wrapped her arms around her sister. "Shh, you're safe now, they can't hurt you."

Kade felt the tight rein Apolly held on her control.

Ali sniffled, then pulled back. "I don't understand. What's happening?"

"I'll explain it all later, but first, we need to take care of Mayara." Apolly stood up, drew in some air, and with a quick glance at Kade, put some distance between herself and her sister.

"Were you bitten?" Kade noted the slice on Ali's arm and the stain on her shirt.

Ali blinked, then shook her head. "No. He ..." She looked down at Mayara, who lay still on the floor. "He's hurt. He killed a couple of them and then got me out of the house. We were on our way here when they cut us off." She stifled a sob. "He saved me, but the—he told me the monsters are called weren—they hurt him badly."

"You got away and we'll take care of Mayara. That's all that matters right now," Kade said, inching slowly closer.

Ali shook her head. "We almost didn't get away. He lost his weapon and we were surrounded. Then another wolf—weren—showed up and they all fought. That's when we slipped away." She glanced down at Mayara, then back up at Kade, eyes wide with remembered horror. "We have to get him to a hospital. He said he needs blood."

"Not that kind of blood," Kade said.

"W-what do you mean?"

Kade didn't answer. "I'd like to check him out, but first, can you give me the weapon?"

Ali stared at the blaster. "I don't know. He told me not to let anyone in here."

Apolly moved up beside Kade and crouched down in front of her sister. "It's okay, sis, I promise. Kade here is one of the good guys."

Ali frowned at her, but lowered the weapon. "You look different."

"Do I?" Apolly took it and handed it over to Kade.

But as Rossa approached, and Ali cringed back again, a look of panic filled her eyes.

"It's all right, sis." Apolly moved to shield her sister from the other hunter. "He's a good guy as well."

Kade passed the weapon back to Rossa, then moved closer to his number one pilot and best friend. "Hey, buddy, can you hear me?"

Mayara's eyes opened briefly. "Kade, I lost my blaster."

That was not good, they didn't need the Earthlings finding alien tech. "It's all right, buddy, we'll find it."

Mayara's eyes slid closed. "Keep Ali safe."

"Can you help him?" Ali asked.

"I'm going to try." But as Kade looked at her, she lowered her gaze.

Kade caught the tears in his new mate's eyes and understood her desire to do more for her sister. Instead, he pretended not to notice and instead checked Mayara's wounds. He looked up at Rossa. "He needs to feed, and we need to get him back to the *Sentinally* ASAP."

Rossa grinned. "I can pilot us."

Kade nodded.

"Feed?" Ali asked.

Apolly squeezed Kade's shoulder. "I can feed him."

Kiss of Darkness

"Why are you talking about food? He's hurt. He needs a doctor," Ali said.

"A doctor can't help him," Kade said gently, then addressed Apolly's comment. "You and I can sustain each other, but your blood won't help him."

"B-blood?" Ali glanced down at Mayara. "I saw ... his teeth." She swallowed hard. "Y-you're vampires, aren't you?"

"Ali—" Apolly started to speak.

"No. I know you like to protect me, but you've never lied to me. Don't start now. I know what I saw. Those weren that attacked us, they're like werewolves, aren't they?"

"Yes, and you're right. Mayara and his friends are vampires, and the ones who attacked you are like werewolves, only they're not from this world." Apolly paused and Kade could feel her need to tell her sister that she was a vampire as well, but she feared her sister's reaction.

Ali stared at her. "And you? You're one of them now, a vampire?"

Apolly nodded.

Ali looked at Mayara. "So, he really needs to drink some blood?"

"He does," Kade said grimly.

Ali bit her lower lip. "W-will mine work?"

"Ali—"

Ali stared at Kade. "If I give him my blood, will that make me a vampire too?"

"No," Kade said.

"Okay, then. How do I give him my blood?" she asked.

"Ali, wait—" Apolly looked at Kade. *What about the sexual part?*

He shook his head. *While our bites can feel good, what you experienced only happens when mates come together, so you need not worry.*

Ali glared at her. "Don't stop me, sis. I know you worry about me, but please, Polly. He saved my life. If I can help save his, then"—she lifted her chin—"then he can have my blood."

Apolly smiled at her. "Ali, I do worry, but honestly, I'm just really proud of you right now. You have such courage."

"Don't say that yet. I haven't actually done it," Ali replied. "I may still freak out or throw up."

Apolly chuckled. "You'll be fine."

10

The Lost Crew

After Ali fed the wounded hunter, Kade tapped his comm unit. "Kellan, status? Any word from Viper?"

"No."

"Helltar!" They'd have to locate the hunter later, along with Mayara's blaster. "How far away are you? We need to get Mayara up to the *Sentinally*, and the sun will rise soon."

"I'm here, though I'm not sure what I'm looking at. Seems to be a sick version of *Twilight* and *Close Encounters*." The warrior growled. "What the hairy grem balls is going on?"

"Wait here," Kade told Ali and Apolly, then he and Rossa went back out to speak with his sister.

Apolly stepped up beside him.

Kade raised an eyebrow.

"What, you think I'm just going to do what you say all the time?" she asked.

"That would get very boring," he said with a little grin.

Apolly smiled, but it faded and was replaced by fear as at least thirty weren emerged from the trees.

A murmur rippled through the new crowd at the sight of Kade. Dread filled him when they all knelt in the dry grass and lowered their heads. "Prince, and Princess." A male at the front spoke, glancing at Kade, then Indris. "We're sorry we failed our mission."

Kade ignored the titles, then stiffened as he recognized some of the males and females from the crew of the *Dadeus*.

Kellan walked past the group, giving them a look of disgust as he joined Kade and his hunters at the shuttle. "Nothing, and I mean nothing, surprises me anymore."

"Get off your knees," Kade directed the comment to the weren, unable to hide his annoyance. They did as he commanded, staring uneasily at him.

Kade looked at his sister. "Indris, what the helltar is going on?"

"You know how Andricans can't be turned?" She cast a glance at the one on the ground.

Kade felt sick as he realized what his sister was going to say. "How is this possible?"

"The *Harbinger* pack figured out a way."

"Why did they call you 'Prince' and her 'Princess'?" Apolly asked quietly, her hand brushing his.

"You didn't tell her?" Indris asked.

"There hasn't exactly been time," Kade snapped, then addressed the weren. "How did this happen?"

"Captain Kade D Kava, my Prince," Sawyer, the former captain of the *Dadeus*, came forward.

"Just call me Captain," Kade said.

Sawyer lowered his gaze. "Right. Please, I beg forgiveness, not for me, but for my crew."

"Tell me what happened."

"The *Harbinger* dropped out of warp and attacked us. We fought. Both our ships were damaged, but theirs more so. They backed off, then landed here on Earth. Since it was our job to protect the humans, we followed."

"The crew of the *Dadeus* fell into the *Harbinger*'s ambush," Rafe said.

"Is that correct?" Kade asked the group in front of him.

Sawyer nodded. "One of the weren seems to have the ability to turn our kind."

"We have to take out the *Harbinger* pack. They need to be stopped," Indris said.

"And we want to help," Sawyer added.

After what the *Harbinger* pack had done to his crew by turning them weren, Kade couldn't blame him. He focused on his sister again. "If Father finds out the truth, they're all dead."

She raised an eyebrow. "Are you going to tell him? 'Cause I'm not."

"We can't just leave a bunch of weren running loose on Earth," Kade said.

"We'll be discreet, and we promise not to hurt any humans," Indris said. "I'll personally see to it."

"We?"

She nodded and lifted her chin defiantly.

Kade gave up trying to get her to see reason, and honestly, he wasn't even sure exactly what that reason might be anymore. Why try to return her to their world where she wasn't wanted just because his father demanded it? Because he'd been trying to keep the peace. Though seeing her now, he finally understood. She was a leader in her own right, just not of Andricans, and she had a mate. "I don't know." He sighed. The whole thing was way too complicated. "Too much could go wrong. We don't need an interstellar war."

"I agree." Indris turned to the crew of the *Dadeus*. "You know who I am. This is my mate, Rafe. Some of you know him as Rafarious, the alpha of the *Raken Claw*. If we claim you as pack, will you recognize us as your alphas?"

Kade glared at her. "Indi, what are you doing? You go too far!"

She smirked at him. "I'm attempting to protect the humans and the crew of the *Dadeus*, dear brother."

Kade wanted to object, but what could he say? Despite the fact she was his sister, and he was expected to return her to their home world and would now have to lie about her whereabouts, she was a grown female. He fought not to smile as she took charge of the newly turned weren. Besides, when had he ever done what was expected?

As one, they all went to their knees again. Then with an arm across their chests, they began to chant. "Indris Electa Kava, and Rafarious Raken, we recognize you both as our alphas and renew our pledge to protect the humans of Earth."

"We accept. Now rise and stand tall," Indris said.

The weren stood.

"I take it you're not going home anytime soon," Kade said.

"Now you're catching on," Indris replied, grinning at Apolly as she slipped her hand into her mate's.

Kade looked at Rafe. "I still don't like it, but so long as you treat her right, I won't object too strongly."

Rafe grinned. "I don't think you have to worry. If I slip up, she'd let me know and put me in my place."

"That she will." Kade eyed the weren on the ground,

remembering why he seemed so familiar. "Do you have anything to say for yourself?"

The weren shook his head. "No, other than I should have killed you when you were a child, and even if you kill me, my pack will take your house down."

Kade glanced at his sister. "What will you do with him?"

"He's dead." Indris smiled in anticipation. "But how fast or slow will depend on whether he tells us where to find his pack."

"Good, anyone who strives to hurt a child doesn't deserve to live." And this particular male, once an Andrican in the emperor's employ, had been a caretaker of Kade's. One of his torturers. "My mate and her sister"—Kade glanced apologetically at Apolly before looking back at Indris and Rafe—"can't go back to their home until the weren who attacked them are all dead. As you know, we have an injured hunter we need to get back to the *Sentinally*, and Viper is MIA. I can give him a few days, but I have a cargo hold of grem that need to be returned to their owner."

Indris pursed her lips guiltily at his stare.

Kade continued. "I'd like your word you won't engage Viper should you find him, or hurt him in any way."

"The sun will be up soon," Indris said. As a half Andircan and half weren, she didn't need to worry about such things.

"I know." Despite how lethal Viper might be and the fact he was a mixed blood, Kade knew the male still couldn't tolerate UV rays.

Kellan started away from the ship. "I'm going to keep searching for him."

"Kell, stop," Kade commanded.

His warrior scowled at him. "He's my brother. I can't just leave him here."

Kade shook his head. "Like Indris said, it'll be daylight soon."

"I can find shelter," Kellan protested.

"No." Kade wasn't about to lose another hunter. "We'll come back for him as soon as night falls again. Besides, Viper is the most capable male I've ever met, he'll be fine."

"We'll help look for him," Indris said. "Give me a comm unit so I can get in touch when we find him."

Kellan looked at her skeptically. "If he doesn't want to be found, you won't find him."

She nodded. "I know, but Rafe and I'll still look. Plus, we've got better noses than you so that might help."

"Fine." Kellan shot Kade a look. "Just as long as you promise that we'll come back as soon as the sun sets."

Kade nodded. "Of course, Viper may not be my blood, but he's my brother."

Without another word, Kellan went into the ship.

"I'll grab another comm unit," Rossa said and followed him.

"We also need our ship back," Rafe said.

"I'll have Nico bring it down." Kade hesitated. "We, ah, took out a couple of your weren when we found it."

Rafe shook his head. "They weren't ours. My crew is all here."

"Then they were of the *Harbinger* pack." Kade felt a bit better about it. If Rafe's crew were the good guys, and they appeared to be, then he didn't want to be killing any of them.

"Mayara won't be happy," Kellan said, as the shuttle took off to fly them back up to the *Sentinally*.

"What won't I be happy about?" Mayara, who they thought

was asleep on the bench seat where they'd placed him, piped up.

As Kade groaned, Kellan scowled at him. "Cap here decided to give the pretty ship back to the weren, we're apparently on the same side now."

"Ah, no." Mayara lifted his head and pouted at Kade. "Seriously?"

"Seriously," Kade said, ignoring Kellan digs. "And just Indris and Rafe's pack."

"Well, I guess that makes sense." Mayara laid his head back down and winced. "Why do these seats have to be so hard?"

Apolly leaned close to Kade. "Are you going to tell me why they called you 'Highness'?"

The crew went silent.

"We'll talk about it when we're alone in our room," Kade said.

Apolly narrowed her gaze on him. "Fine, in our room."

Kade caught Ali studying him. "You're safe, little one. No one here or on board the *Sentinally* will hurt you, I promise."

Ali watched him for a moment, then looked at Apolly. "When can we go home? I need my computers. I have a game I'm launching soon."

Apolly winced. "I'm afraid we won't be going home until the rest of the weren who attacked you are taken care of."

"I'll get whatever you need tomorrow night," Mayara said.

Ali glanced at him in surprise, then slid her sweatshirt off. "Here, put this under your head."

After a brief hesitation, Mayara did as she said and then smiled. "Thank you, Ali."

Apolly's sister lowered her gaze, but not before Kade noticed the pink filling her cheeks.

Once on board the *Sentinally*, they transported Mayara to

Belsuma in the med bay. As she checked Mayara over, she glanced at Kade. "Lieutenant Kelseyann called. We've updated her on what's happening. She was about to head here to see you." Belsuma glanced at Apolly, then turned back to Kade. "I told her you'd call her instead."

Kade nodded, gave Mayara orders to get some rest and recover, then led Apolly and Ali to a room close to theirs. "I hope this room will be adequate?" he said to Ali as the door slid open.

She walked in, gazed around, then looked back at them. "Where will you be?"

"Right next door," Kade said.

"Okay."

"I hate to leave her," Apolly said once they were back in Kade's—no, their room.

"It's been a long night, she needs to rest," he said as the door closed behind them.

"I know. I just feel bad, this is all my fault. Those weren wouldn't have gone after her if it wasn't for me." Apolly wrapped her arms around herself.

"Come here." Kade started to pull her against him, something he'd been wanting to do since the minute they left his room earlier. As someone not used to touching others, it surprised him that he was so easily able to do so with Apolly, though he wasn't about to question it.

Apolly moved away instead. "Who's Kelseyann?"

"Kelseyann? She's just a friend."

Apolly raised an eyebrow. "Friend?"

"Yes, a friend," he said firmly. "I've known her since we were kids and you have nothing to worry about regarding her, trust me."

Apolly stared at him, then nodded. "If you say so, then I

will."

"Good, because I've never felt like this with anyone but you." But Kade could still see the worry in her eyes. "Tonight wasn't your fault. You didn't ask the weren to attack you, or that little girl. But if you hadn't been there, I guarantee they'd have turned her and used her, badly. You saved her life."

Apolly moved close and finally leaned into him. Then she wrapped her arms around him, and it felt good. Right. Like he'd finally found home. "Do you really believe that?"

"I do," he said, rubbing his chin in her hair and inhaling her scent.

"You knew that injured weren, didn't you?" Apolly let him go and went to sit on the bed. "And you definitely didn't like it when the other group called you 'Prince.' Why? Who are you and why didn't you want to tell me?"

Kade sat beside her, his heart thumping in his chest. He didn't know when it happened, but he'd fallen for Apolly hard. "Because you're my soulmate and I love you, and I'm terrified you'll hate me when you find out who I am."

"Soulmate?" Apolly blinked. "Wait, you ... love me?"

"I do. I think I fell in love when I first saw you fighting and taunting the weren. You were so incredibly sexy, and coming from me, that's saying something."

"Well, good then." Apolly pulled his mouth down to hers and kissed him.

Kade groaned, then almost cried when she pulled away.

"This is really kinda crazy, we've only known each other a night." She stared at him. "Yet, I feel the same about you. But you have to start talking. Tell me who you are. I want to know who I've tied myself to. What exactly are soulmates, and how are you so sure that's what we are?"

"Soulmates are two halves of a whole, and they are forever.

They can feel it deep inside, they complete the other person in a way no one else ever can."

"So, this Kelseyann?"

Kade smiled. "I told you, she's just a friend, and I think you'd like her."

"Not likely if she has any sexual designs on you," Apolly said, then seemed to be mulling the rest of it over. "Are you going to explain about everything else?"

Kade took a deep breath. He'd never spoken of his childhood to anyone, and Indris only had the slightest idea of what he'd gone through. But Apolly was right, if they were going to have any sort of life together, he needed to tell her. "That weren Indris and Rafe captured used to be Andrican. He was also one of my more ruthless caretakers when I was a child. My father wanted his son raised in a *certain* way, and Cain Orvey exceeded his expectations in training me."

Apolly ran a hand down Kade's arm, hating the agony he tried to hide. Whatever he'd been through had been bad.

"He did things to ... toughen me up." Kade paused. "You have to understand us as a race first. Andricans don't feel anything at another's touch, other than pain. We can feel pain. We can also have sex, but it's emotionless and definitely not like what we did earlier, unless it's with our soulmate. So because of that, a lot of Andricans as they age mentally—we don't age physically—they crave the ability to feel something. Some grow to embrace pain, either submitting themselves to it, or inflicting it on others. Cain Orvey liked to hurt others. He got off on it, and loved to experiment on me first."

"I'm so sorry, Kade." Apolly snuggled closer and wrapped

her arms around this male who'd touched her heart in a way no other man ever had.

"It's all right, it ended when I turned sixteen and refused to join my father's army."

"Army? Who is your father?" Apolly could feel Kade's hesitation.

"My *father* is the Andrican emperor Joem Artes Kava, of House Kava Artemis."

"An emperor?" Apolly tried to wrap her mind around it all. Vampires, royalty ... "I've heard of the goddess Artemis from my grandmother, but the rest means nothing to me." She looked at him. "So you're a prince. I can see it, you're very handsome."

"No, I'm not a prince. I'm a hunter." Kade got up and began to pace. Finally, he stopped and faced her. "I don't follow my father. I left and never looked back. I don't agree with him or his practices. My crew and I are hunters. We go after the vilest creatures in the universe."

"Okay, so your father is an asshole. Lots of parents are."

Kade raked his fingers through his hair, then faced her again. "My father just happens to be one of the worst around. Thousands of years ago he claimed Earth as his."

Apolly blinked. "Thousands of years ... how old is he? Wait, he claimed Earth?"

Kade nodded, looking like he was sure she'd hate him now.

Apolly could never hate him. She patted the bed beside her. "Sit and tell me what you mean."

Kade sank back down beside her and explained it all.

"And your father sees us humans as his property, to feed from?" Apolly asked, sick at the idea.

Kade nodded but didn't look at her.

Apolly gently cupped his face. "Kade, do you believe as your father does?"

"No. Never. That's why I went my own way. I want nothing to do with him or his empire."

"Then you have nothing to fear. I'd never hold what your parents do or believe against you," she said softly.

Tortured eyes met her gaze.

Apolly smiled. "I do have something to tell you, though."

Kade waited.

"My father was human, but my mother was only half human. Her mother, my grandmother, is the goddess Apollamina, and I inherited a few little gifts from her, so did Ali," she said.

"That explains why you were able to keep me out of your head," he responded.

"I felt you pushing at me." She laughed, then pulled him close for another kiss.

This time when she withdrew, it was to stand and slowly peel her clothing off.

Kade got rid of his, and as she joined him on the bed, he lowered his lips to hers once again. *I'll never get enough of you.*

Good, 'cause I love you, my alien vampire. *Now hurry up and show me how much you love me.*

Thank you for reading Kade and Apollo's story. If you enjoyed it, I'd very much appreciate if you could leave a review where you purchased it.

Read on for a sneak peek of Hunting Darkness, Book 2 in the Alien Vampire Series.

11

SNEAK PEEK HUNTING DARKNESS

Hunting Darkness
Chapter One

Hungry Hunter Hunting

Planet: *Terra Nova/Earth to the Earthlings*
   Location: Los Angels, California.
   Time: The Present

As a hardy, long-lived race from another world, Viper should have healed within minutes, if not seconds. But as he walked, moisture trickled down his side. His clothes stuck to his skin, itchy and uncomfortable. How he'd love a redo on taking out the furry beast once again. The weren had lucked out when he got hold of Viper's blaster and turned it on him. Only this time, Viper would make the creature's death slow. And painful. It was too damn bad that the freaks dissolved into vapor when they died. He clenched his jaw as his glyphs activated.

This wouldn't have happened if it had been Viper's DNA-coded blaster. But it hadn't been. That particular piece was waiting to be fixed. Without thinking, Viper had grabbed one they'd pulled off the grem—a species of nasty rat shifters—ship when they rounded up the vermin. It was stupid—he knew better than to bring along an unfamiliar weapon without trying it out first. Yet it had belonged to Jace, a fellow hunter they'd lost when the grem shot him out an airlock.

They got control of the situation, scuttled the ship, and confiscated all the weapons. Most were junk, but amid all of it, they found a familiar one: Jace's.

Viper thought nothing of using it. Sure, it wasn't programmed to his DNA specifically, but he and Jace both had Andrican blood, so it would still work.

Nope! Wrong.

He hadn't considered that the grem might have stripped the coding from it, allowing it to work on anyone. The rats weren't normally that smart.

Which meant a weapon that shouldn't have worked on Viper, did.

And he was walking proof with a wound that wasn't healing very fast, if at all. Still, it took more than this to kill one of his kind. At least his comm unit deflected some of the blast.

Viper tried not to dwell on it, but it wasn't easy. Each step he took sent pain shooting through him, and it didn't help that his glyphs were acting up. He didn't think it was due to the wound but had no clue what else it could be. Well, that might not be entirely true. He had a couple of ideas, one of which seemed ludicrous.

He should be heading to meet his fellow hunters—his

brothers. Instead, he was many miles from where they were supposed to rendezvous. If his comm unit worked, he'd have called in. To top it all off, he'd even lost his ear unit. Seemed that it was one of those nights.

At least things couldn't get worse, could they?

And even if his communication unit did work, would he have called in? Viper didn't know, which was a bit embarrassing. He was never indecisive and had never been one to be led around by his balls. Yet here he was, following some sort of compulsion, a drive to a destination unknown.

His brothers would never believe it.

This whole thing was a problem, and Viper kept those to himself. It was a trait he'd learned early in life. Keep quiet, observe, and most importantly, beware of who you trusted. Those were the ones to betray you.

Not that he thought his brothers would.

Yet, it was not easy to dismiss those early lessons when they were the reason he survived hell and kept his brother alive.

Jaw clenched, Viper turned down another deserted street. He kept going partly to quench his curiosity at what was pulling him in that direction, though anger played an even bigger reason. The compulsion to obey infuriated him.

It didn't help that this compulsion seemed entwined with a scent that stirred his blood in a way he'd never dreamed possible. He'd heard the stories of this happening to his kind before but had never believed them. He had a strong will and could easily disregard it. In fact, he'd done so earlier. But it caught him again, and now he needed to find whatever it was and stop it.

He'd covered many miles—a hungry hunter hunting those targeting Earthlings.

At least the trick-or-treating appeared to be over. Most of

the humans were safe inside their homes. Goody for them. If they knew what stalked them at night, they'd never come out of their houses.

Though he and his brothers were tired and hungry, not stopping here on their way to Beltin 1 Orian—where they planned to rest, feed, and have a bit of fun—hadn't been an option. At least not for Kade, Viper's captain.

Had it been up to Viper, though, well, he held no love for humans or most other species.

Of course, that was one of many reasons he wasn't the captain and didn't command a crew.

Still, he could have removed himself from the mission. Yet, with a chance to exact revenge on an enemy, how could he decline? Besides, his brothers—one literally, the others figuratively—were all going. And since they were the only beings in all the galaxies he gave a shintila about, he couldn't let them go alone.

Sure, his captain saw it as saving the Earthlings from whatever the helltar the weren were doing, but Viper honestly didn't give a fuck about the planet or its inhabitants.

He and his brothers were hunters. And they were damn good at their jobs—tracking down the scourge of the galaxies. The fact they got paid very well for it didn't bother him one bit. Retrieval jobs were more of a pain in the ass, but so long as they got their spending credits, he didn't care.

But this mission? Viper was pretty sure they wouldn't see a single cred for it.

So for the first time in his forty-eight years, Viper found himself on Earth. He only wished it were under better circumstances—say, like the ban forbidding human contact had been lifted. But that wasn't the case. For some reason, the weren—

Kiss of Darkness

wolflike beasts, only larger and often uglier—decided Halloween was a good night to play with Earthlings.

A scream pierced the night.

Viper caught a familiar snarling and growling. Weren, likely attacking some helpless Earthling. He glanced around, but no doors opened. No one came out to see what was happening. Of course, half of these places were dilapidated and probably empty.

Next came the begging, crying, and whimpering.

At least no one but him, with his exceptional hearing, would catch the horrible noises.

Goalendamn weren. Why were they fixated on the humans?

Viper sighed. He was all out of antivenom after using the last to save a couple of kids who'd been bitten.

The wise thing would be to ignore the compulsion, get to the rendezvous and see if they had more, and come back. If not, then someone would have to head up to the ship and retrieve more. Either way, it would be too late.

Viper went straight for the ruckus, which seemed to be coming from an underpass. Made sense, the beasts preferred the shadows.

Viper and his fellow hunters had hoped they were chasing the *Raken Claw*, but what they'd found tonight raised their suspicions. The *Raken Claw* couldn't be doing all this. Which begged the question, how long had the weren been here? Why Earth? What were they up to?

Sure, the beasts were still killing humans, but they were also turning them, something they didn't generally do. The weren were a very insular race, their packs tight-knit, and from what he'd learned over the years, they were extremely particular in who they turned—who they admitted to their packs. They chose only those who'd benefit their race or keep their females safe. Which often resulted in a lot of strong, and often psychopathic, weren.

Not much that Viper witnessed tonight made sense. He might not like them, but unlike the grem, the weren weren't stupid creatures. Earth was off-limits. Every alien in all the galaxies knew it.

No, something was up, and Viper and his brothers had to figure out what. Only then could they get back to their original plans. The crew was due for a break, but they couldn't leave Earth infested with the vile creatures.

Not unless they wanted to see a war in space, and that wasn't something Viper would wish on anyone. Not even if it were the only way to stop the top powerhouses.

Earth's inhabitants would be horrified to discover their role in things—that they were *owned* and considered nothing but food by the Andrican emperor. Though there wouldn't be much they could do about it. With a larger fleet than any other royal house, House Kava Artemis was the most ruthless and feared.

Viper knew firsthand the devastation war could induce, and as memories tried to surface from a past he refused to think about, he shoved them away.

He didn't care—he couldn't.

Yet, he did worry about the fallout of what might happen here. As a planet listed as off-limits, the hunters' presence held serious repercussions. It may not matter that they'd come to help.

As he caught the scent he'd been following, Viper's fangs ached. He needed blood. They all did. Kade said they could feed after they'd taken care of this weren problem. But Viper would be surprised if his brothers did so. Even if it wasn't forbidden, to partake of human blood—the richest in all the galaxies—was dangerous. It could sink the strongest Andrican into bloodlust. Good thing he and Kellan, his blood brother, weren't fully Andrican.

That was the only perk of their creation.

Fear of getting sucked into bloodlust aside, there was still the fact that just touching an Earthling held a death sentence.

You'd think it would help that their captain was the son of the Andrican emperor, but it didn't. That relationship was a volatile one, and none of the hunters wanted to find out how their captain's sire would react.

The emperor wanted his son to fall in line—be another pawn in his army. Kade refused. So, though they came to Earth to help eradicate the weren problem, Viper didn't believe they'd have any protection.

With his traitorous blaster in one hand and blade in the other, Viper hurried down the broken and cracked sidewalk, avoiding the weeds and garbage that littered the street.

He hugged the shadows and silently crept closer to the underpass. Neon graffiti, symbols, and characters he didn't recognize covered the concrete, and up above on the road, an occasional car passed by.

ABOUT THE AUTHOR

Sheri-Lynn Marean is a Canadian Author of paranormal fantasy romance with kickass heroines, sexy beasts, mystery, suspense, and twists you won't see coming. Her main series is The Dracones; Cursed & Hunted. **www.sheri-lynn-marean.com**

Made in the USA
Columbia, SC
06 July 2025